Peacemaker

JAMES SWALLOW

2 4 6 8 10 9 7 5 3 1

First published in 2007 by BBC Books, an imprint of Ebury Publishing.
A Random House Group Company.

This paperback edition published in 2008

Doctor Who is a BBC Wales production for BBC One
Executive Producers: Russell T Davies and Julie Gardner
Series Producer: Phil Collinson

The Random House Group Ltd Reg. No. 954009.

Addresses for companies within the Random House Group can be found at
www.randomhouse.co.uk.

A CIP catalogue record for this book is available from the British Library.

ISBN 978 1846076312

The Random House Group Limited supports the Forest Stewardship Council
(FSC), the leading international forest certification organisation. All our titles
that are printed on Greenpeace approved FSC certified paper carry the FSC
logo. Our paper procurement policy can be found at
www.rbooks.co.uk/environment

Series Consultant: Justin Richards
Project Editor: Steve Tribe
Cover design by Lee Binding © BBC 2007

Typeset in Albertina and Deviant Strain
Printed and bound in the UK by CPI Cox and Wyman, Reading, Berkshire

For Colin Ravey

The sun rising over the top of the distant mountains made them shine like polished copper, and Matthew Belfield held up a hand to shield his eyes from the glow. He felt a grin tugging at the corners of his lips and let it come. Was this going to be a good day? He wanted very much for it to be so. Things had turned so hard and sorrowful over the past few months, but finally, after everything that had happened, after all the trials he and his wife had faced, Matthew was daring to hope that their lives were taking a turn for the better.

He blew out a breath, resting a moment across the top of the fence post he'd been fixing since the pre-dawn light. He stood there in the valley and listened to the quiet of the place.

It was the quiet that had made him pick this parcel of land to build their homestead on. Matthew remembered it clearly, climbing off his horse and wandering out across the plain for the first time, just walking. Just *listening*. It was like… Well, it was like he could hear the breathing of the earth itself, the gentle noise of the wind through the grasses. It was then he knew he was going to spend the rest of his life in this valley, carving a future out of the rough lands of the West.

He turned slightly and looked back at the house. Celeste moved past one of the windows, not seeing him, a water jug in her hands. She'd be making a draught of tea for them both once the stove was stoked, and then maybe some breakfast. Matthew was pleased to see his wife on her feet again, walking around and laughing like she used to. It was almost as if the sickness had never touched her. She was well and whole again; the woman he'd married back in Boston was with him once more. *It's a blessing, Matthew Belfield,* she had said only the night before, *we were touched by our own little miracle, right here in the middle of these here wilds.*

He found himself nodding. For a moment, Matthew thought of how sickly she had seemed, before. He saw it in his mind's eye; Celeste there on the big bed in the back of the house, lost in the crumpled sheets. Her skin as pale as milk, her breathing laboured and shallow. He shuddered and his throat felt tight. Matthew dared not think how close the good Lord had come to taking her away from him for ever, and he promised himself that he'd do whatever he could to make sure no harm befell his wife again, not as long as there was still a breath left in his body.

If not for *him*, if not for that travelling man, why then Matthew would be staring not at the woman he loved but at her grave in the shadow of his house. The stranger had come from out of nowhere, drawn, so he said, by word from the folks in the town up along the valley. Oh sure, he seemed a mite peculiar, and maybe there was a way about him that in other circumstances would have flagged him wrong; but he'd done what he said he would. The fella hadn't asked for much, not much at all when you weighed the price against the life of Matthew's wife. And in return, he'd brought about a cure that had healed all of Celeste's ills in a day. A single day! The thought of it still amazed Matthew; but he wasn't a man to question good fortune. If providence had brought the stranger and his companion to the Belfield homestead, then who was a simple farmer to argue against it? Celeste's life had been put to rights, and that was about East as far as her husband was concerned.

She glanced out of the window and saw him looking back, threw him a smile. He tipped his hat in a shallow howdy, but as he did he saw the smile slide away from his wife's face. She was looking out past him, off down the range.

Matthew turned and stared out the same way. He saw the sign immediately, the wispy curls of trail dust etching up from the dirt road. Horses, then. Two of them, if he didn't miss his mark, and they were coming at a pace like the devil himself was at their heels.

The farmer drew himself up and straightened. They weren't expecting any company, and out here in the wilderness it wasn't the manner of things to have a neighbour turn up at your door, not without good cause. Matthew tapped the pocket in his waistcoat where his Bowie knife was concealed. It never hurt to be prepared.

The riders slowed as they approached the Belfield house and for a moment Matthew thought he heard a sound like a swarm of flies buzzing; but the air was too cool of the morning for insects to be up and around, and he narrowed his eyes.

He studied the new arrivals and right away he felt unsettled. The horses they rode were of plain stock and he didn't know the brand upon them, but they were damp with sweat and both animals were breathing hard. He chanced a guess that they'd been ridden swiftly for miles and with little care or attention for their wellbeing.

The riders, though; they were men the likes of which Matthew had never seen. They were gaunt figures, the pair. Long coats all dark and tight upon them, with a faint air that hung around which recalled rotting meat, or old, dried blood. It wasn't a scent to be treasured. Under wide, flat preacher hats that cast deep, inky shadows over their faces, he could make out grim expressions and sallow skin.

With a quick flourish, one of the men dismounted and Matthew caught a glimpse of a long eagle feather trailing from the back of the man's hatband. He landed firmly with a clink of spurs and was still. For a brief moment the homesteader's gaze dropped to the finely tooled gun belt that rode low on the man's hips. A heavy iron-grey weapon sat there in a fast-draw holster. Matthew found it hard to look away from the pistol. Even at rest, the sight filled him with a cold fear.

He licked his dry lips and cleared his throat. 'This land is my property. Might I ask what it is you gentlemen want hereabouts?'

'Looking,' said the rider, after a long moment. His voice was thick with an accent that Matthew couldn't place. 'Looking for a thief.'

'Is that right?' Matthew moved slowly, putting himself between the house and the pair of longriders. 'Well, you're lookin' in the wrong place. We're law-abiding folks here, Mr, uh…' He trailed off.

The man on foot seemed to think about it for a moment, as if he needed to draw the information up from a great depth. Finally, he pressed a thumb to his chest. 'Kutter,' he said, by way of introduction. He nodded at his companion on horseback. 'Tangleleg.'

The farmer forced a smile. 'Well, Mr Kutter, might I be correct in assuming you all are both regulators or of a like, in search of the bounty on a man?' When neither one spoke, he pressed on. 'I can assure you, there's no outlaws in these parts. The wife and me don't have any truck with lawbreakers.'

Tangleleg spoke for the first time, and his words

were sharp and dry, like the sound of bones snapping. 'Where is the healer?'

Matthew's blood chilled in his veins. 'Who?'

Kutter's left hand brushed the grip of his pistol and the homesteader saw something glitter there on the weapon, like tiny glowing embers. 'We know he was here,' said the longrider. 'We can see his track. Where is he?'

'Where is he now?' added Tangleleg. 'Answer.'

His hands bunched into fists and Matthew took a breath. *Who were these two highbinders, to come on his land and make demands of him?* Anger took the place of his fear. When he thought of all the things he owed the stranger who had helped his wife, he was damned if he was going to give him up to the first roughneck who demanded it. 'I don't know no "healer",' he snapped, 'and if you know what's best for you, you'd be on your way, or else—'

Kutter's gun came out of its holster in a flicker of steel, almost as if it had leapt from the leather into his waiting hand. The weapon blurred toward Matthew and he recoiled. Kutter aimed the barrel at the farmer's chest, the muzzle never wavering even a fraction of an inch.

Matthew blinked, standing his ground. The gun was *huge.* Bigger than a Colt .45, thickset and cut from fluted sections of steel and brass and what might have been bone, it looked utterly lethal. Kutter held it without concern, but it seemed so dense and weighty that

Matthew wondered how the man could hold it without using both hands.

'Answer,' repeated Kutter.

From behind him, Matthew heard the well-oiled click of a shotgun hammer; and then the voice of his wife. 'You heard my husband. This is Belfield land. You're not welcome here, so get yourselves gone.'

He used the moment to step back, turning. Celeste was at the door, the long ten-gauge shotgun at her shoulder. She was shaking slightly.

Kutter spoke as if he hadn't heard a word she had said. 'This is the last time we will ask you. Where is the healer?'

'He ain't here,' said Celeste. 'Been gone for a couple of weeks now.'

Matthew nodded. 'That's the size of it.' He put his hands on his hips, trying to show a little backbone. 'That there fella? We don't care what he mighta done to incur your displeasure. Fact is, the man saved my wife's life! We don't know where he's gone to, and if we did, then we sure as hell wouldn't tell you!'

Tangleleg shook his head slowly. 'You are lying. We can see it in your face.'

Kutter mimicked the other man's actions. 'We can hear it in your voice.' He moved again, another sudden rush of motion from complete stillness.

Celeste saw this and with a start she jerked the twin triggers of the double-barrelled shotgun. Thunder spoke across the homestead and Matthew heard a cloud of buckshot whistle past him. Kutter was blown off his feet and into the dust. He dropped, but the big pistol never left his grip.

Matthew expected Tangleleg to draw, but he didn't. He remained motionless, sitting high in his panting horse's saddle, watching them.

And then Kutter got up.

Not without pause, but he got up unaided. The longrider brushed at his coat with his free hand and shook off the flattened specks of spent lead pellets. He paused, using his thumb and forefinger to pick out the odd piece of shot from the ashen skin of his cheeks.

Celeste gaped. The man should have been dead, or at the very least at the door to it. Instead, Kutter behaved as if she'd hit him with nothing more than a wet rag.

'You are a waste of our time,' said Tangleleg.

The rider's pronouncement was pitiless. Matthew saw Kutter move again, this time a blur of dark clothing, and then a bolt of lightning flew from the muzzle of his weapon into the wooden walls of the house. The blast knocked both the Belfields off their feet as a ripple of fire flashed out across the cabin, shattering the windows and setting everything alight. Matthew struggled to get back to his feet, lurching toward the porch where his wife had collapsed in an untidy heap.

On his horse, Tangleleg mirrored his companion's actions and drew a pistol, fired a spread of shots into the house. Unlike the flat crack of a bullet, each discharge came with a tortured scream of sound and the tang of hot ozone, acrid like the air before a storm front. Blazing blue-white beams stabbed out, ripping the house into pieces.

Matthew gathered his wife to him as both longriders found their marks. His last thoughts were of Celeste and of how much she meant to him; and of the man who had saved her, if only to give him these few more days in her company.

White fire ripped into them, turning their flesh into ashes.

The longriders remained for a while, enough to give the flames time to take purchase and ensure that nothing would remain of the Belfield homestead. The horses grew skittish and whined at being so close to the fires, but the men did not move at all. They stood, their heads tilted back slightly so that their mouths were open, allowing the fly-buzz sounds from deep in their throats to resonate through the air. It was a quicker and far more expedient manner of communication than the more clumsy use of teeth and lips and tongue. Together, they consulted maps made inside their heads, looking for new signs, for likely bolt-holes and targets of opportunity.

When their next destination was decided, Kutter went to get fresh horses from the stables beyond the ruined Belfield household, while Tangleleg killed their old mounts. After a meal of raw meat, the longriders rode on, heading westwards.

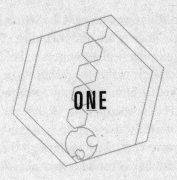

ONE

As they walked down the neon-lit boulevard, Martha Jones looked up to see the hazy, glowing arc that bisected the night sky over their heads, twinkling against the alien starscape beyond it. It reminded her of a snowfall, but suspended in the air like a freeze-frame image. She blinked and laughed in delight as she realised that there were actually letters imposed on the shimmering band. She picked out a 'W', an 'O' and then another.

'*Woo!*' she said, reading it aloud. 'Ha! Doctor, look! It says "woo" up there! That's funny.'

The Doctor halted and gave her a lightly mocking *can't-I-take-you-anywhere?* sort of look. 'Actually, we're only just seeing the end bit of it. The whole thing says "*Hollywood*", but the letters are a hundred-odd kilometres high and you have to be in polar orbit to read it all at once.' He made a circling gesture with his index finger. 'Rings, you know? Like Saturn has in your solar system. Made of ice and rock dust. The owners use photomolecular field generators to hold the letters in place. It certainly makes the planet easier to find.'

She smirked at him, raising an eyebrow. 'There's a planet called Hollywood? Planet Hollywood?'

'Yup,' He started walking again, hands in the pockets of his big brown coat, skirting through the thronging mass of variant life forms who were also out enjoying the warm evening.

Martha was still looking upwards. 'Oh yeah, the letters are moving, I can see it. Now it says "*Ood*".'

'That's an entirely different planet,' he said offhandedly. 'This one was terraformed in the late twenty-fifth century by a consortium of entertainment businesses, right after the Incorporated Nation of NeoCalifornia was finally destroyed by a super-volcano.' He pointed up into the sky. 'There's also BollyWorld in the next orbit over, a bunch of Celebra-Stations…'

'What happens there?'

'It's like a safari park, except you get to chase no-talent android celebrities around instead of wild animals.'

Martha made a face. 'Things haven't changed much in 400 years, then.'

He went on. 'This place is the movie capital of the Milky Way, and it's got the best cinema anywhere, anywhen…'

She nodded, taking it all in. 'When you said we could go to the movies, I had thought, y'know, we'd stop off at my local multiplex or something…' Martha dodged to one side, to allow a pack of cheetah-girls in opulent holographic dresses to pass them.

The Doctor turned to face her, walking backwards. 'Well, we could. But this place has really smart seats.' He moved seamlessly, never once bumping into anybody despite the fact he wasn't looking where he was going. 'And I mean really smart, as in *intelligent*. They mould to all your comfort zones, but not so much that you doze off during the good bits. And there's no sticky floors or people talking during the film. Free popcorn as well.'

'Choc ices?'

He nodded. 'Oh yeah. All the trimmings.'

Martha gave him a sly smile. 'Ooh, cosy. It's almost like a date.'

For a second, the Doctor was slightly wrong-footed. 'No, not really. Just, uh, two mates, going to see a flick…' He cleared his throat and pointed in the direction of a low dome made of hexagons a short distance away, changing the subject. 'They copied the design from a place on Earth, the Cinerama on Sunset Boulevard.' He waved at the roof. 'I've had a soft spot for it for ages. Defeated an incursion of Geomatide Macros there back in the 1970s. Nasty things, they used the angles of the ceiling tiles as a mathematical hyperspace vector generator…' He trailed off and then clapped his hands. 'Right! What do you want to see? They've got everything. *Pirates of the Caribbean VI? The Starship Brilliant Story? Casablanca?*'

She sighed. 'I'm in the mood for a Western.' The words popped out of her mouth without her thinking about it. 'I haven't seen one in ages.' And suddenly, Martha felt a little bit sad. 'When we were kids, me and Leo and Tish, we'd watch a cowboy film every Sunday afternoon. There was always one on, just before lunchtime. Mum would be cooking a joint and making these great roast potatoes, and we could smell it from the living room. We'd all get together, the three of us and Mum and Dad, and eat during the last half.' She sighed. 'Funny. It seems like that was a very long time ago. A very long way away.' Martha thought of her family and if felt like there was a vast, yawning distance between her and them. A pang of homesickness tightened in her chest, and her eyes drifted up to the alien sky again.

'A Western it is, then,' said the Doctor gently. '*Rio Bravo. A Fistful of Dollars. Dances With Wolves...*' He fell silent as they approached the box office. The kiosk was dark and lifeless. 'Hang on. This doesn't look right.' He fished in his pocket and aimed his sonic screwdriver at the booth. The slender device buzzed, and the door hissed open. He glanced inside and gave a pained groan, returning with a moment later with a sheet of electronic paper in his hand.

'What's wrong?'

'Cinema's closed,' he replied, showing her the paper. 'It seems that last week they were having a disaster film festival, using virtual-environment simulators. Apparently, someone set the dial too high when they were screening *Earthquake!* and, well… The floor caved in.' He sighed. 'Still. Better that than *The Towering Inferno.*'

She turned and walked back the way they had come, back toward the TARDIS. 'It's OK. Never mind.' It was odd; after all, it wasn't as if they were talking about anything serious, right? It was just a *movie*, wasn't it? And yet Martha felt cheerless, as if something as simple as being able to watch some creaky old Wild West film was the only way she could feel close to her family, out here in the depths of space-time, so far away from all she knew.

The Doctor trailed behind her, stepping up to unlock the door of the police box as they returned to the alley where it had materialised. He seemed to sense her change of mood. 'I'm sorry, Martha.'

She tried to make light of it. 'Oh, who wants stale popcorn and runny ice cream anyway?' But she couldn't keep the disappointment from her voice.

They entered the wide, domed chamber of the control room, stepping into the thrumming heart of the TARDIS.

All at once, the Doctor's expression changed. He grinned. 'You know what? You're right. And I have a much better idea.'

He bounded past her to the console that ringed the crystalline central column. Without any apparent order to his actions, the Doctor skipped from panel to panel, flipping switches and spinning dials.

He paused, chewing his lip, and then worked a crank handle.

Martha's momentary melancholy faded before his burst of excitement. She had to smile; the Doctor had a way about him, as if he took each piece of sadness in the universe personally, like he had sole responsibility to banish the gloom from things. 'What are you up to now?'

He peeked at her from around the column. 'Why bother *watching* the Wild West?' he asked her. 'Why bother watching it when we can, well…'

'Go there?' Her smile widened.

The Doctor grabbed the TARDIS's dematerialisation control. 'Martha Jones,' he said, slamming the lever down, 'Saddle up!'

Jenny hitched up her skirt an inch or two so she could cross main street without getting more than a speck of mud on her. She picked her way around the trestle tables and makeshift chairs set up along the boardwalk outside the Bluebird saloon.

A couple of the bar girls gave her a respectful smile and a wave, pausing in their work. They were putting up some bunting to string along the storefronts, in preparation for the street party that evening. Jenny smiled back and kept on her way, stepping up past Vogel's General Store. Held in a bundle by a leather belt, the books she carried were an awkward burden, and she had to keep stopping to adjust them so they didn't fall. They were a precious cargo; there was little enough reading matter hereabouts, and Jenny felt like it was her duty to keep as much of it safe and secure as she could.

As she passed the jail, the sheriff stepped out, taking a draw from a thin cigarillo between his lips. He saw Jenny and tipped his hat. 'Good morning, Miss Forrest.'

'Sheriff Blaine,' she replied, bobbing her head.

'And how's the day been treatin' you, might I inquire?'

She showed him the books. 'I've had a minor windfall. After Mr Toomey's passing, his widow donated these to the schoolhouse library.'

Blaine nodded. 'The sour old fella was good for somethin', then.' He eyed the books. 'Myself, I never been blessed with an over-abundance of schoolin', but I see the merit in it.'

'His passing was a sad matter.' She sighed. 'I suppose we must thank providence that more didn't follow him.'

'Toomey was never a fit man,' Blaine noted. 'If the sickness was gonna take anyone, I would have wagered it'd be him.' The lawman took another drag on the cigarillo and blew out smoke. 'I reckon we've been blessed to lose so few.'

Jenny shifted uncomfortably. 'That is one way to see things, I suppose.'

Blaine showed a crack-toothed smile. 'Heh. If you'll

pardon me sayin' so, Miss Forrest, but I've never been clear why it is a woman as fair and as educated as yourself finds it so hard to see the good in things.'

She frowned. 'I'm just… just cautious, is all.'

'Well, I hope that won't stop you comin' along to the festival tonight. Gonna be a talent contest outside the Bluebird, a potluck and singin'. Just what folks need, after what happened.'

Jenny moved on. 'Perhaps I will,' she told him. 'I have some work to prepare for the children's lessons tomorrow. Perhaps, if I get finished in time.'

Blaine tipped his hat again and walked off. 'Hold you to that, ma'am.'

She left him behind, turned the corner and ventured down the side street; and for a brief instant a peculiar noise came to her on the breeze. Jenny couldn't place the sound at all. It was like, oh, the grating of a pair of giant bellows, or the rasping of a winter wind through the trees. It seemed to be issuing from the alleyway behind the Assay Office.

The schoolteacher hesitated for a moment, her caution warring with her curiosity. But as usual, caution won. She shook her head, dismissing the moment, and carried on her way.

The Doctor closed the TARDIS door behind him and took a lungful of the morning air. 'Smell that?' he asked. 'That's history!' He sniffed. 'Ooh. And someone frying grits, if I'm not mistaken.'

Martha wandered up to the mouth of the alley, and she smiled broadly as a man rode past her on a black mare. 'You know, every time we land somewhere I think I'll get used to it, I'll be blasé about the whole thing…' She turned back and laughed. 'But I'm not. I can't be. This is it. We're really here!'

He shared her smile. 'We really are.'

There were clapboard buildings on either side of the road, shallow single-storey stores and offices made of rough-hewn wooden planks, some with grassy sod on their roof, others with heavy shingles. She saw an uneven sidewalk made of cut logs, horses at hitching posts outside, and men and women in period costume going about their business. *But they're not in costume, are they?* Martha shook her head, answering her own question. *This isn't like some Disneyland-type theme park playing at being the Wild West, this is the real thing.*

The Doctor joined her, licking his thumb and holding it up to the air. 'This is 1880-something, I reckon. A Monday. Just after breakfast.'

'How can you tell that?'

He gave an offhand shrug. 'Ah, you know. It's a talent.' He nodded at the street. 'C'mon. Let's have a wander.'

The town had an unfinished look to it, with tents here and there, houses that were half-built and others that were clearly brand new and unweathered by the elements. Martha saw signs for a bakery, stables and a tannery. There was even a post office, with a telegraph cable looping away from a tall pole outside the building.

She glanced left and right, taking it all in. 'Look at me. I feel like such a tourist. I wish I'd brought a camera.'

The Doctor chuckled. 'Really? And what would you tell people when you showed them the pictures?'

Martha caught sight of a storefront with a sign that read 'Undertaker'; outside there were four pine caskets, each one propped up and open with a shrouded body visible inside. She looked away. 'I'd tell them it's not like it is in the John Wayne movies.'

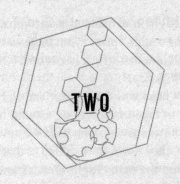

TWO

The teacher adjusted the bonnet on her head and picked up her pace, still turning Blaine's words over in her mind. In all honesty, Jenny Forrest wasn't much for dancing, although she enjoyed the playing of a piano when the mood struck her; but, try as she might, she found it hard to conjure an upbeat mood in the wake of what had happened in the township. It seemed like she was the only one who dared to dwell on it. Everyone else was going about their business as if nothing had happened, afraid to talk about it.

Jenny shook off the moment of introspection and became aware of a couple walking ahead of her, talking animatedly. It was their accents that immediately took her attention; English, the pair of them.

One was a tall, wiry man in a long brown coat, without a hat upon his head, wandering along the street with his hands buried in his pockets. At his side was a dark-skinned girl in an oxblood jacket with a wild shock of hair. Jenny couldn't place it, but there was something about the clothes that struck her as odd. *New styles from the East Coast, perhaps?*

The girl's head was darting left and right, as if she was trying to take in everything around her. 'This is amazing,' she was saying. 'The Wild West. Wow.'

'Actually, they don't start calling it that for a long time yet,' said the man. 'Right now it's known as the "New West". Because it is. New, I mean.'

'Think of all the places we could visit!' enthused the girl. 'The Alamo!'

'We're a few years too late for that.'

'Deadwood?'

He shrugged. 'The people there are very rude…'

'How about… Tombstone, Arizona? The gunfight at the OK Corral!'

'Been there, done that.' He gestured around. 'Anyway, what's wrong with this place? What's wrong with, um…' The man turned and spotted Jenny walking behind them. He gave her a wan smile. 'Hello there! This might sound like a silly question, but, uh, where are we?'

Jenny coloured a little, feeling slightly embarrassed about listening in on their conversation. 'This is Redwater. You're new to the town, then?'

'Oh, yes,' said the man, grinning. 'Very new. Brand new, even.' He offered her his hand and she shook it. 'Hello! This is my friend Martha Jones, and I'm the

Doctor.'

She smiled back. The man's open manner was infectious. 'Miss Jenny Forrest, at your service. A pleasure to meet you, Miss Jones, and Doctor, uh—'

'Just Doctor,' he replied. 'Redwater, is it? Splendid! I love the place names in this part of the world!'

Her brow furrowed. 'I didn't know we had new arrivals. The stagecoach from Dekkerville isn't due for another week or so.'

'We, uh, rode in,' said the girl. 'In a manner of speaking.'

'Of course.' She studied the man. 'Doctor, while it is always stimulating to have someone of learning visit our township, I must confide to you that if you've come having heard of our epidemic, your journey has been wasted.'

'Epidemic?' Martha's smile froze.

'Really?' replied the Doctor, shooting a quick glance at the girl. 'And why is that?'

'The sickness was cured.'

Martha eyed her. 'What sickness would that be, then?'

Jenny held the books closer to her chest. 'Why, the smallpox, of course.'

Being a gentleman about things, the Doctor offered to carry Jenny's books for her and she took them to the clapboard schoolhouse at the far end of the street. The teacher insisted on making them both a cup of tea as a thank-you, and when she was out of earshot Martha leaned close and spoke in an urgent whisper. 'Smallpox?' She was all business now, the carefree traveller part of her put away and the trainee medical doctor at the fore. 'If there's been an outbreak here, these people could be in serious trouble.'

'But she said it was cured.' The Doctor's doubt was clear in his tone.

Martha shook her head. 'Uh-uh. Smallpox doesn't get eradicated for almost another hundred years yet.' She shuddered. As part of her training, Martha had been educated on how to identify and diagnose infectious diseases, including ones that were technically extinct. She remembered the pictures she had seen of victims of the virus – scarred by lesions all over their bodies, blinded or partly paralysed. And those were the lucky ones, the ones who had survived exposure. 'Vaccinations weren't very widespread around now...'

'No,' agreed the Doctor, thinking. 'Not at all.'

'So the disease might not be gone. This could just be a lull, an incubation cycle.' She thought of the bodies at the undertakers. If the infection was still lurking in them...

'Smallpox was a deadly killer in the nineteenth century,' he noted. 'Outbreaks were quite common... Sometimes whole communities were wiped out by it.' He jerked his head toward the schoolhouse's window and the town beyond. 'But this place doesn't look like somewhere in the aftermath of a plague, does it? No funeral pyres, no mass graves or houses burnt down to stop contamination. It's just…'

'Too normal?'

He nodded 'Yeah.' The Doctor's smile snapped back on as Jenny returned with cups of strong black tea. 'Oh, thank you.'

The schoolmarm sat with them and untied the bundle of books. 'It's the least I can do for visitors. Tell me, do you have lodgings? I can recommend Mrs Lapwing's boarding house just over yonder.'

'Thanks,' smiled Martha.

The Doctor helped Jenny with the books, sorting through them. 'Ah, *Twenty Thousand Leagues Under the Sea!*' He waved a volume in the air. 'This is a great one.'

The teacher cocked her head. 'Indeed? I have not read it, but I have found Mr Verne's other scientific romances to be most thrilling.'

'Jules took a lot of convincing to cut out the stuff about the Silurians.' He handed it to her with a wan smile. 'Still a great romp, though.'

'*Doctor,*' Martha put a little edge in her voice, bringing him back on track. 'Perhaps Miss Forrest can shed some more light on what we were just talking about?'

'Oh, call me Jenny, please,' said the woman. 'Did you have a question?'

He took a breath. 'The sickness you talked about. You said it was cured.'

Jenny nodded. 'That's quite correct, although the manner of it was beyond me.' She frowned. 'Frankly,

Doctor, and as a learned man I'm sure you would agree, it has always been my estimation that those who pose as miracle workers are nothing of the sort.' She got up and walked across to a cabinet on the wall. 'Every encounter I have had with men who peddle these so-called patent cures, these powders or philtres for what ails you, they have all been nothing more than confidence tricksters…'

'But?' said the Doctor.

The teacher sighed. 'He came into town a couple of weeks ago, in a gaudy wagon with an Indian youth as his travelling companion.' She pointed out into the street. 'He set up a stand across from the Bluebird saloon. At first he did magic tricks, silly parlour prestidigitation and that sort of thing. He used a lot of long and complicated words to dazzle the less educated members of the community.'

'You're talking about a medicine show,' said Martha. 'Like a travelling salesman. Con artists, really. Quack doctors with made-up cures that do more harm than good.'

The Doctor glanced at Martha. 'The Western equivalent of a guy trying to get you to buy rubbish double glazing or knock-off DVDs.'

Martha's jaw hardened. She took her career as a doctor as the most serious thing in her life, and the thought of people playing at the job, making things worse instead of saving lives, made her quietly furious.

'On any other day, he would have been run out of

town,' Jenny continued, 'but the Lesters, they'd come down with a powerful malaise. So this man, who went by the name of Alvin Godlove, he ignored the red flag outside their house and went inside, bold as brass. And that night, the Lesters were up and about, as well as you or I.'

'Is that so?' The Doctor threw Martha a look. 'But the Lesters weren't the only sick ones, were they?'

She shook her head. 'The contagion had touched a lot of folks, truth be told. But Godlove made them all well again, and pretty soon everyone in Redwater was lining up to buy a bottle of his remedy from the Indian.'

'That's… quite a story,' Martha said carefully. 'An overnight cure for smallpox.'

Jenny took a bottle of liquid from the cabinet. 'I must confess, despite all my misgivings about the man, in a moment of weakness I purchased a measure of the solution myself. Not that I was infected, mind, but I thought it best to have some in the schoolhouse's medicine cabinet. Just in case.'

'Can I see?' The Doctor took the bottle and examined it. There was a crudely printed label gummed to the outside. *Professor Alvin Q. Godlove's Powerful Dispatulated Incontrovertible Panacea Potion – For All That Ails Man or Beast! Promised to Recover Potency, Aid the Retainment of Hair, Banish Illness and Inoculate Against All Forms of Croup, Grippe and Sickitude.* Thin liquid sloshed around inside the container. He took out the cork, sniffed it and made a face. 'It's a bit whiffy.'

'We've heard tell that Godlove has worked the same miracle all over the county.' Jenny sat down across from them. 'But still I find it difficult to put aside my prejudice about the gentleman.' She grimaced. 'He was a lewd sort, if you take my meaning.'

'Shameful,' said the Doctor, peering into the bottle. 'Miss Forrest… Jenny. Could I borrow this for a bit? I'd like to give it a closer examination.'

'You believe you could fathom its secrets?'

He stood up. 'I'll have a go.' He nodded to Martha. 'Why don't you stay here, finish your tea? I'm going to pop back to our, uh, transport.' He flashed Jenny a smile and made for the door. 'Enjoy the book. The bit with the squid is *great*.'

As the door slammed, Jenny nodded after him. 'Your Doctor has an odd turn to him, if you don't mind me saying.'

Martha chuckled. 'Trust me, you don't know the half of it.'

He ran the test using the molecular sensor pallet in the TARDIS control room, tipping a little of the fluid from the bottle into the scanning tray. It took about ten minutes to get the results, and when he read the printout the Doctor shook his head and crumpled it into a ball. *Wrong.* That had to be wrong. He did the test again. And then a third time.

He fished out the creased ball of paper from where he had thrown it, smoothed it out and laid it next to the two others. He put on his glasses and looked again. All identical. All wrong?

There was a way to be sure. He uncorked the bottle and gulped a mouthful.

'*Ugh*.' It was greasy, and it made his throat sting a bit. 'Why does medicine, no matter what planet you're on, always taste disgusting?' Sour-faced, the Doctor licked his lips. 'OK. Grain alcohol. Some chocolate in there too, I think. A lot of sugar. Water. And, ugh. Rock salt. *Yuck*.' He wished he'd brought some of Jenny's tea to wash the taste away.

He held up the bottle to the light, the glow of the TARDIS filtering through it. 'This,' he said to the air, 'is about as medicinal as a bucket of cheese. The only thing you'll get from this is rotten teeth.'

But if that was true, then how had Alvin Godlove used it to save an entire town from a lethal epidemic?

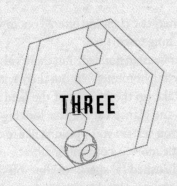

THREE

When Jenny mentioned the words 'street party', some of Martha's earlier good mood returned to her and, with firm but gentle insistence, she made the young schoolmarm agree to act as her guide to Redwater. Martha played the role of tourist, allowing Jenny to slip into her role of teacher, nodding with interest as she gave her a potted history of the township. Redwater was in the Colorado Territory, a long ride south from the city of Denver, and the place had got its name from the ruddy colour of the earth that bordered the thin stream running alongside the settlement. Jenny's explanations took on a slightly stiff tone as she explained that the redness came from a preponderance of iron in the local hills. Martha smirked; Jenny was a teacher all right. She couldn't help lecturing.

She looked up as they approached the small crowd gathered in the main street. Music from fiddles and a chorus of energetic clapping filtered out towards them. 'This is a mining town, then?'

The other woman nodded. 'But there's also farmland in the valley and homesteaders out there with grain and cattle. We take up the bounty of the land as we can.' She paused and glanced at Martha, looking her up and down. 'Are you certain you wouldn't like to change into clothes a little more… conventional?'

Martha brushed a speck of lint off her jacket. 'Something wrong with this? It's my favourite. Got it in a sale at Henrik's.'

Jenny coloured a little. 'It's just that… Well, in these parts dress is sometimes more conservative than you might be familiar with.'

She eyed the teacher's long, broad black dress and shook her head. 'I wore something like that a while ago. Wasn't really my style, if you know what I mean. I'm OK with my jacket and jeans.'

'Of course,' Jenny replied. 'I didn't mean to be rude.'

Martha's smile widened as she imagined how the woman would react to a browse around the clothes stores on Oxford Street. 'I bet you'd look brilliant in a miniskirt and a crop-top.'

'A crop top,' repeated Jenny, sounding out the words. 'What an interesting name. Is it like a bustle?'

Martha grinned. 'Kind of, yeah.'

Jenny was quiet for a moment. 'The Doctor… Is he your patron?'

'What, like my boss? Hardly!' She smiled. 'At times

he might think he's in charge, but that's not how we work. We're travelling companions, I suppose you'd call it.'

The teacher's cheeks reddened in a blush of embarrassment. 'Oh. *Oh*. Pardon me, I didn't mean to pry into your affairs.'

Martha held up her hands. 'It's not like *that* either,' she said quickly, before the other woman got the wrong idea. She let out a sigh and her shoulders sank slightly. 'It's not like that at all.'

A group of children ran past them, calling out a hello and Jenny waved back at them. 'Some of my charges from the school,' she explained.

The boys and girls ducked around the adults, laughing and giggling. Jenny explained that the kids were engaged in a game of something called 'Pom Pom Pull Away', but Martha soon gave up trying to follow the rules. It wasn't just Redwater's younger citizens who were having fun and entertaining each other; as the two women walked past the Bluebird saloon, a pair of men with bow fiddles were tapping out an upbeat song about some lady called 'Sweet Betsy' and, as they came to a conclusion, the crowd roared approval. Without pause, the musicians launched straight into another tune, and Martha gasped as she recognised the rhythm.

'Cotton Eyed Joe!' She laughed and clapped her hands. 'I know this one! My dad used to play this every time we had a Christmas party, that horrible drum-

and-bass remix version that goes on for ever…' Martha trailed off as Jenny looked at her blankly. 'Ha. Never mind.'

'Everyone certainly does seem to be enjoying themselves,' said the teacher, and Martha heard the wary edge in her words.

'And why the heck shouldn't they?' They both turned at the sound of the new voice and saw a portly, florid-faced man with a bowler hat poised at a rakish angle on his head. 'Today's a celebration of life, an affirmation!' He nodded to himself.

Jenny inclined her head in greeting. 'Mr Hawkes, how are you?'

'In fine fettle, Miss Forrest!' He shot Martha a sidelong glance. 'Have you taken in a domestic? I wasn't aware.' The man had a bundle of printed papers under one arm.

'This is Martha Jones,' said Jenny. 'She's a new arrival to our fair town. She's travelling with her associate, the Doctor.'

Hawkes grunted. 'A Doctor, you say? Well, doesn't that beat all? We don't see a single medico in Redwater for nigh on a year, then two of them turn up within a week of each other! What are the odds?'

'Just lucky, I guess,' offered Martha. Hawkes glanced at her and then looked away, back to Jenny. Her lip curled as she realised the man was ignoring her.

'Our noble lawman Sheriff Blaine told me he'd spoken with you today,' he continued. 'He expressed the opinion that you were in a mode of distress and ill-ease, by his measure.'

'I assure you, I am thriving,' Jenny countered.

'As are we all,' Hawkes said, with an expansive wave of his hand, 'thanks to the miracle of recent days... But no, I believe his meaning was toward your inner manner, not any outward sickliness. He said, if you will permit me to say, that you appeared gloomy.'

The teacher bristled. 'I would have said thoughtful.'

Hawkes gave a patronising laugh. 'Aha, and therein lies the problem! I would hazard that a fine young woman like you ought not to busy her pretty head with doubts over things that are already done and gone! Instead of searching for a rotten fruit among the bushel, why not enjoy the apples you have?' He nodded again, pleased with himself.

'Indeed,' said the teacher, and she nodded at the papers under Hawkes's arm to change the subject. 'Is that the new edition?'

'Certainly is!' He unfurled one of the sheets and offered it to her. Martha realised that it was a newspaper; a masthead with *Redwater Chronicle* written in fancy lettering dominated the top of the page. Beneath it were the words 'Zachariah Hawkes, Editor in Chief and Publisher'.

'Ooh, can I see?' Before Hawkes could protest, Martha took it from him and scanned the document. It was just a single sheet of rough yellow paper, with smudged lines of thick, large text.

Hawkes stuck out his chin and spoke directly to Martha for the first time. 'I'd have my doubts someone of your persuasion could read it, let alone understand it.' He gave a disdainful sniff.

Martha pointed at the paper. 'You've spelt "Kansas" wrong, there and there. And "government". And "illustrated".' She pulled a mock-sad face. 'Would you like me to spell-check the whole thing for you?'

The man glowered at her and snatched back the paper. 'If you'll excuse me,' he grated. 'Clearly there was a mistake with the printing press I was not aware of.' Grumbling, he stalked away.

Jenny sighed. 'I apologise for his rudeness. He was brought up in the south, you understand? His family owned a plantation and many, uh…'

'Slaves?' Martha said the word without weight.

The teacher frowned. 'When President Lincoln outlawed that barbaric custom with his emancipation proclamation, it did not sit well with some,' she admitted. 'One would think that as we approach the turn of the century, mankind would become more enlightened.'

Martha gave a rueful smile. 'We can only hope.'

The other woman was quiet for a moment. 'Martha, would you like to try something sweet? I know the very thing.'

Jenny guided her over to a stand near the general store and bought them both a piece of biscuit-like cake dipped in honey.

And sweet it was; Martha's eyes widened when she took a bite. 'That's terrible!'

'You don't like it?'

'No! I mean it's terribly good! And probably very bad for me!' They shared a laugh and polished off the treats in silence.

Martha licked the last of the honey from her thumb and eyed Jenny. She wanted to keep the mood light, but the truth was, every time she looked around and saw the people clapping, singing, and being happy, she couldn't help but be drawn back to the schoolmarm's grim words about the smallpox outbreak. Something about it all seemed... *forced*.

People did not get well from a virus like that overnight, not in a place and a time like this. Maybe if the TARDIS had arrived at some point in the far future, or on some alien planet, she could have accepted it – but this was the Wild West, the 1880s. People had only just caught on to the idea of these invisible things called *germs* that made you sick. A super-cure for smallpox didn't exist in 2008, so how could it exist here?

'A penny for your thoughts,' said the teacher.

'I was going to say the same thing to you,' admitted Martha. 'Look, sorry to bang on about this, but what you said before, about the sickness...'

She nodded. 'It troubles me, and clearly my concerns have been noted by others.' Jenny looked in the direction of the newspaperman's office. 'I hate to be thought of as some kind of Doubting Thomas, but while everyone applauds our good fortune I cannot help but be worried by it.' She gestured around at the street party. 'All of this… It's just a circus to keep the townsfolk from dwelling on the matter as I have. A few bawdy songs and some honey cake, and they forget their fears. They move on as if nothing has happened.'

'But you can't do that,' said Martha.

Jenny shook her head. 'Perhaps Hawkes was right. Perhaps I am just a gloomy soul, looking the gift horse in the mouth, finding fault with our good luck.'

'There's no harm in asking questions,' Martha retorted. 'One thing I've learned travelling with the Doctor is that the moment you stop questioning things, that's when trouble starts.' She smiled faintly. 'Life challenges us, doesn't it? We should challenge it right back.'

The teacher nodded. 'I agree. But there are plenty of people in Redwater who feel very differently. They're afraid, you see? Superstitious, I suppose you could call it. They're good people, but they're scared. They're terrified that if they dwell on what happened, then somehow they'll undo it all.'

'They think the disease will return?'

Jenny nodded again. 'And if it does, we will all fall victim to it.'

Martha was about to say in no uncertain terms exactly how ridiculous an idea that was, but before she could open her mouth a tall guy with a scraggly beard and a dirty brown jacket came racing up to them. He was panting hard, and he had that kind of wet-dog smell on him that people who work with animals always have.

'Miss Jenny,' he puffed, bobbing his head to the teacher, and then belatedly to Martha as well. 'Miss Jenny! I'm glad I found you so quick-like.'

'Joseph, what's the matter?'

The man hesitated, then pivoted and offered Martha his hand. 'Apologies, Miss, Joe Pitt at your service,' He showed a quick flash of broken teeth. 'Nice to meet ya.'

'Mr Pitt owns the livery stable across from the school,' Jenny explained. 'Joseph, is something awry?'

The man swallowed. 'Just came into town, passing the schoolhouse.' He pointed back in the direction they had walked. 'Big window at the front, it's been stove in. Broken all abouts, Miss Jenny.' He blew out a breath. 'And I reckon there might be a fella inside there.'

Jenny gathered up her skirts. 'Joseph, thank you kindly for coming to me with this.' She grimaced. 'This would not be the first time someone has broken in, believing mistakenly that there's wealth to be had in the schoolhouse.'

'I can come with and help you corral whatever roughneck might be makin' trouble back there,' Joe offered, squaring himself up.

'Please do,' said Jenny. 'Martha, perhaps you ought to remain here.'

Martha glanced around; there was no sign of the Doctor. For a moment she considered racing back to the TARDIS to look for him; but then she rejected the idea. 'Let's all go,' she said firmly. 'Three of us against one burglar? No contest.'

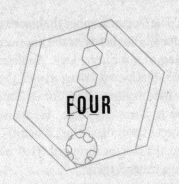

FOUR

The Doctor placed both hands on the saloon doors at the entrance to the Bluebird and pushed them open with a jaunty flick of his wrist. They flapped open and closed, open and closed, and he stood watching them, beaming.

'Brilliant,' he said aloud, reaching out to flap the doors again. 'These are great! And they're going to have such a big comeback in the 1970s, believe me. You won't be able to walk into anyone's kitchen without going through a set of these.' He puffed out his cheeks and wandered into the saloon proper, taking it all in. He walked in what seemed like an aimless course, finally ending up at the bar. 'Hello!' he said brightly, addressing the small fellow in the apron tending the customers. 'You know what, I'm parched. I suppose a cuppa is out of the question?'

'Just what you see,' came the surly reply.

'Oh-kay,' The Doctor scanned the blackboard behind the bartender's head, between the big mirror and the lurid painting of a reclining lady. 'Applejack, Redeye, Gut Warmer, Blackstrap.' He read out the names of the various hard liquors. 'Dust Cutter, Tonsil Varnish, Sudden Death, Tarantula Juice.' He paused. 'Is that made from real tarantulas? No?' When the bartender said nothing, the Doctor shrugged. 'How about a glass of sarsaparilla instead, then?'

The man in the apron grunted and went to get his drink. A few steps down the bar, a man in a broad-brimmed hat and black waistcoat gave the Doctor a sneering look. 'Sarsaparilla? Maybe a glass of milk would be more to your likin', English.'

'Milk does a body good,' replied the Doctor. 'Although you're off about the "English" thing. Funny coincidence, actually. Same accent, different stellar cluster.'

The bartender plonked the drink down in front of him. 'That'll be a bit,' he demanded.

'A bit of what?'

'One bit,' growled the man and he held out his hand. 'Twelve cents!'

'Oh, money!' The Doctor nodded, and fished in his pockets, pulling out pieces of string, a yo-yo, a pencil, a Japanese bus timetable and his sonic screwdriver. He paused. 'Ah. I think I may be, what's the term for it? Temporarily financially embarrassed.'

The bartender reached out to take back the drink,

but the waist-coated man stopped him. 'Leave it, Fess. Put it on my tab.'

The Doctor saluted him with the glass. 'That's mighty neighbourly of you.'

The other man picked up the sonic screwdriver before the Doctor could sweep it back into his coat pocket. 'Strange-looking contraption. Bet it's worth a buck or two.'

'Or three,' he said carefully.

The man touched the brim of his hat with a finger. 'Name's Loomis Teague. I'm known hereabouts.'

'I'm the Doctor,' he replied. 'I'm, uh, not.'

Teague weighed the sonic in his hands. 'Tell you what, Doc. How about you return my goodwill with a little sport?' He nodded in the direction of a table where a group of men were sat over fans of playing cards. 'Join us for a game?'

The Doctor lowered his voice. 'Like I told Fess there, I am a bit cash-poor at the moment.'

Teague's fingers curled around the sonic screwdriver. 'Reckon this'll serve just fine as your grubstake.'

'That has... sentimental value,' he replied. 'I'd rather not part with it.'

But Teague was already walking away. 'Guess you better have an affinity for the cards then, Doc.' Loomis took an empty seat and, as one, all the other players gave the Doctor the same predatory look. Teague pushed a chair out with his boot. 'Plant your backside, Coney. We'll go easy on ya.'

The gamblers all smirked with harsh humour as the Doctor joined them. 'This is great,' he enthused. 'I was hoping to find someone to have a chat with, and here we are, with you nice fellows inviting me over to your table.' He rubbed his hands. 'Excellent stuff!' There were a pile of careworn playing cards lying in front of him, and the Doctor gathered them up. 'Um, sorry?' he asked. 'Before we get started… What are we playing? Happy Families? Snap?' He peered at the cards and a grin burst out on his face. 'Oh, wait, I know this game. It's Top Trumps, isn't it?'

Joe's description was dead on; the pattern of the glass fragments showed how the window had been forced open. Martha didn't wait for Jenny or the stableman to go first. She saw a spatter of bright blood on the wooden lintel and took the initiative, stepping through into the darkened schoolhouse.

Martha didn't allow herself to worry that there might be something dangerous in there; bloodstains meant that someone had been hurt, and injured people were her priority. She went in boldly. 'Hello? Who's there?'

The blinds had been drawn, making the room shadowy. She stepped around the pieces of broken glass and saw a shape huddled in the far corner, between a desk and the blackboard. Behind her, Jenny and Joe were following.

'I'm Martha,' she said, keeping her voice clear and even. 'Have you hurt yourself? I can help you.' She spotted dots of blood leading toward the slumped figure. 'Hello?'

She moved carefully around the desks and saw the shape was a teenage boy. He was panting and shaking, his brown hair plastered to his pale, sweaty face. He was clutching his right hand with his left. Martha recognised the symptoms of a panic attack immediately.

'Nathan?' The youth looked up as Jenny spoke his name. 'This is one of my former pupils. He helps me with the younger children and such,' she explained. 'Nathan, what happened here?'

The boy got shakily to his feet. 'I… I cut myself. I'm real sorry…'

Martha saw the laceration across the teenager's palm. 'Let me see that,' She took his wrist, and with a handkerchief from her pocket she set to work cleaning up the cut. 'This looks a lot worse than it is.'

'Were you here stealing?' demanded Joe. 'When your daddy hears about this—'

Jenny held up her hand. 'There's no need for that. I'm certain Nathan has an explanation.'

The boy looked up at Martha and she saw fear in his eyes. 'I came looking for the teacher… Needed to find somewhere safe.'

'Safe from what?' Martha asked gently, tearing the handkerchief into a makeshift bandage.

Nathan tapped at his temple. 'I can't close my eyes, miss. Each time I'm abed, I see 'em.'

Joe shifted uncomfortably. 'The kid's addleheaded

over somethin'. I'd reckon he's up to some dare with those other young reprobates, that's all.'

But Martha knew real terror when she saw it. The boy was deathly afraid of something. 'What do you see, Nathan?'

He shuddered and Jenny answered for him. 'It's the night terrors.'

'No such thing!' snapped Joe, but he didn't sound like he believed it.

Martha shot him a look. 'Sounds to me like you're trying to convince yourself, not him.' She guided Nathan to a chair. 'You're having bad dreams, is that it?' She chewed her lip; she wasn't trained in psychology, but she'd try her best.

'He's not the only one,' said the teacher darkly.

The boy blinked. She could see grey rings under his eyes from where he hadn't been sleeping well. 'The same dreams, over and over. Sounds like shot and shell.' He took a shuddering breath. 'Screamin'. And things walking like menfolk, but with too many arms and legs, faces like things from Hades itself. Some made of iron, others like lizards or birds. Lightning spilling outta guns instead of bullets. Blood-red clouds like giant mushrooms, fillin' the sky.' Nathan looked away. 'Like war, it is. War across the world, only it ain't no world I know.'

Martha's blood ran cold. Someone from the twenty-first century would have said they had dreamt of laser weapons and nuclear explosions, aliens and robots, but Nathan had no idea what those things were; he was describing things beyond his understanding, trying to express something he had no frame of reference for.

'Nothing but flim-flam and tomfoolery,' growled Joe.

Jenny glared at the stableman. 'You can ignore it all you like, Mr Pitt, but it won't go away.'

All at once the stableman grabbed Nathan's arm and tugged him away. 'Come on, boy! I'm taking you back to your daddy to answer for this damage you did!'

'Oi! Leave him alone!' Martha tried to intervene, but Joe was twice her size and pushed her back effortlessly.

'Stop!' shouted Jenny. 'I don't want him punished!'

'Too late for that, now!' said Joe. 'He'll pay you back for the window, count on that. His father will see to it.' He propelled Nathan out of the door, and paused to glare at Martha 'And if you know what's good for you, girly, you'll leave well enough alone!' The schoolhouse door slammed behind him.

'Girly?' Martha turned angrily on Jenny. 'What did you mean about *he's not the only one* and *it won't go away*? Come on, tell me! Why did Nathan break in here like that?'

The schoolteacher began to pick up the pieces of broken glass. She sighed. 'Nathan was one of those who fell ill with the smallpox before that snake-oil salesman came to town. Godlove's medicines healed him and all the others... But ever since the boy's had those terrible nightmares. Visions like hell itself.' She looked away. 'I pray for him every day, but the lad's torture revisits him time and again. I think the schoolhouse gives him some measure of calm. He came here to get away from his dreams.'

Martha's anger faded. 'And others as well? It's not just Nathan who has them?'

Jenny shook her head. 'Several of Godlove's patients suffered the same. But they keep silent for fear of the sickness returning.' She met Martha's gaze. 'I ask you, what kind of cure leaves that in its wake?'

Martha had no answer to give her.

The Doctor looked over the large pile of poker chips in front of him and smiled warmly. 'This *is* going well for me, isn't it?'

The last of the other gamblers threw down his hand of cards in disgust. 'Too rich for me. I quit.' He got up, leaving just the Doctor and Teague in the game. At the other tables in the Bluebird, people's attention had slowly come to centre on the Doctor's unbroken winning streak. All eyes were on him.

He toyed with his cards. 'So, you were telling me about this Alvin chap and his medicine show.'

Loomis Teague frowned, peering at his own diminishing pile of chips. The Doctor had started off by winning back his sonic screwdriver and hadn't let up, alternatively taking the gambler's money and quizzing him about recent events in Redwater. 'Like I said, first off we were thinking he was just sellin' snake-oil and promises, but he made good.'

'How exactly?' said the Doctor, fanning his cards. 'And I'll see your bet and raise you.'

Teague matched his opponent's ante and shrugged. 'Him and that Pawnee sidekick of his, name o' Walking Crow. Went into the sick folk's houses, gave 'em that patent panacea. Next day, they was well again.'

'That simple, eh?' The Doctor raised his bet again. 'I'd like to meet this Professor Alvin Q. Godlove in person.'

Teague's mood was turning more surly by the second. 'Not till we make an end to this,' he snarled, and pushed the rest of his winnings into the middle of the table. 'I'm all in. You gonna match that?'

'In for a penny, in for a pound!' The Doctor copied Teague's gesture and put in all his chips. 'This is exciting!'

Teague's revealed his cards with a flourish. 'Four of a kind!' He went for the pile.

The Doctor shook his head slightly. 'You know, when Wild Bill Hickok was shot in Deadwood, he was playing cards, and he had a fantastic hand! It's a shame he never got to play it.' He smiled and laid down the Aces of Spades and Clubs, followed by an Eight of Clubs, Eight of Spades and Jack of Diamonds. 'Aces and Eights,' said the Doctor, with a mock-sinister voice. 'The Deadman's Hand!' He reached for the chips. 'That would make me the winner, then.'

Teague exploded with rage. 'You dirty four-flusher! You rigged the damn game, coming on like some Coney when you was a card-sharp all along!'

The Doctor frowned. 'Cor, sore loser or what? Come on, don't be a big girl's blouse about it.'

Suddenly there was a wicked-looking buck knife in Loomis's hand. 'Nobody makes a fool outta me—'

'Quit it!' Another figure hove into view, and the Doctor saw a man with a sheriff's tin star on the lapel of his jacket place a firm hand on Teague's shoulder. 'Simmer down.'

'This crow-bait's a cheat, Sheriff Blaine!' snarled Teague. 'Check his pockets! He's gotta have a holdout in there, aces up his sleeves or somethin'!'

'Perish the thought,' said the Doctor.

Blaine eyed him. 'So you're this Doc I been hearing about, eh? Tell me, is Loomis right? You got a deck of cards on you I should know about?'

The Doctor spread his hands. 'I don't know. I might have. I've got very deep pockets. You never know what you'll find in there.'

'Let's take a look-see.' The lawman bent forward and plucked a thin wallet out of the Doctor's coat. 'What have we here?' He flipped it open and his expression darkened.

'What does it say?' demanded Teague.

The sheriff tossed the wallet back to the Doctor with a scowl. 'It says he's a Pinkerton Agent, that's what. A private investigator.'

The Doctor picked up his psychic paper and nodded sagely, playing along. 'That's right. I'm just passing through. Doing, you know, investigating.'

'How can y'all be an investigator *and* a doctor?' snapped Teague.

'I wear many hats,' he replied. 'Well, obviously at the moment, I'm not wearing a hat at all, but you know what I mean.' He picked up the poker chips. 'Maybe I *should* get a hat, actually.'

But his emerging smile froze when Blaine leaned closer and gave him a hard, threatening stare. 'I don't give a horse's backside what you are,' he growled. His voice was loaded with menace, and low so only the Doctor could hear him. 'But if you and that little missy keep asking questions and buttin' in where you ain't wanted, nothin's gonna stop me runnin' you outta town.'

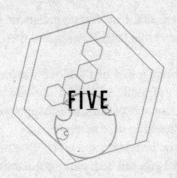

FIVE

Martha leaned against the TARDIS central console with her arms folded across her chest. 'Nathan was terrified,' she concluded, coming to the end of her description of what had happened in the schoolhouse. 'And that big lunkhead Joe didn't help matters any by dragging him off.'

'Mmm.' The Doctor nodded, his concentration on the computer screen extending out of the console panel. He fiddled with the dials and switches underneath it.

Martha pouted. 'Have you been listening to me?'

'I pay attention to everything you say and do, Martha Jones,' he replied, without looking up at her. 'I don't even need to look at you to know you're doing that face.'

'What face? I'm not doing any face.'

'Yes you are. The *moral indignation, how dare they do that, just wait 'til I get my hands on them* face.' He glanced at her and nodded. 'Yeah. That one there.'

She sighed. 'OK, I am feeling indignant. But I've got a right to. First that loser Hawkes and then that smelly stable-guy…'

'What about me? I had a bloke waving a knife at me and an unfriendly sheriff in my face.' He sniffed. 'Mind you, that sort of thing does happen to me a lot. I suppose I should be used to it by now.'

'But maybe he'll leave you alone if he thinks you're a… What did you call it? A pinky-something?'

'A *Pinkerton*,' the Doctor corrected. 'From the Pinkerton Agency.'

Martha grinned. 'Sounds like a dating service.'

'Private investigators and bodyguards, actually,' he told her. 'The Agency is still around centuries from now, in hundreds of solar systems. They had a bit of a rep back in the West, y'see. They always got their man.'

'I thought that was the Mounties.'

'Yeah, them too. But I get the feeling the old psychic paper could tell Sheriff Blaine I was President Grover Cleveland himself, and he'd still give me the bum's rush.' He finished working the controls and stood back, staring at the screen. 'There. That should do it.'

She moved so she could see what he was doing. The screen showed a topographical map of the local area, with clusters of dull yellow dots that had to be people, shifting around like glowing ants.

'What's this?'

'Psychic resonance scan,' announced the Doctor, tweaking a dial to fine-tune the display. 'Looking for telepathic waveforms or esper field projections. Any abnormal phenomena.'

'Like mind control? Is that what you think is going on around here?'

He blew out a breath. 'Small community, unfriendly natives, weird happenings. In my experience it usually adds up to the same kind of thing. Sometimes there's an alien thingy buried under a church or giant cockroaches on the prowl or—' He broke off. 'Well. Let's just say, I'm covering all the bases.' The scanner gave off a desultory ping and his face fell. 'Eh? That's not right.'

Martha tensed. 'You've found something?'

'No. That's just it. I *haven't* found something. Anything.' He frowned and walked away, over to the panel where the brown medicine bottle was standing. 'Curiouser and curiouser.'

'So what's making Nathan and the other healed people have those nightmares?'

The Doctor picked up the bottle and studied it closely. 'I have no idea.' A crooked smile appeared on his lips. 'Isn't that interesting?'

Martha made the face again. 'The word I would use is disturbing,' she said firmly. The Doctor was so fascinated by anything out of the ordinary, but sometimes he needed reminding that normal people were caught up in it. 'If that potion is as fake as you say it is, then something freaky is definitely going on here.'

'There you go, straight to the heart of the matter as usual,' he nodded briskly, slipping the bottle into his pocket. He pointed at her. 'So, on the spot, then. Pop quiz, Doctor Jones. You've got your patients, you've got your mystery symptoms. Grab your stethoscope and tell me what's next.'

She hesitated, following his suggestion. Martha thought it through, as if it was a problem case turning up at the Royal Hope Hospital where she studied. 'Examine the patient. Determine the nature of the illness. Look for vectors of infection. Make a diagnosis.'

'Bingo!' called the Doctor. 'So what we need to do is—'

A sharp double knock at the TARDIS doors sounded out, stopping him in mid-speech. He twirled the monitor and tapped a button so the screen displayed an image of the scene outside. Over his shoulder, Martha saw Jenny Forrest standing in the alleyway in the fading daylight. As she watched, the schoolmarm knocked on the doors once again. Jenny looked concerned.

'Company!' said the Doctor. 'I'll put the kettle on.'

'We can't let her inside!' retorted Martha. 'She'll never get her head around it!'

'You did.'

'Yeah, but I've seen lots of sci-fi movies! She's just a—'

'A what? A nineteenth-century yokel?' He eyed her. 'Prejudice can cut both ways, you know. Just because these people don't know what a cell phone or the internet is, it doesn't mean they're dumb.'

'It's not that,' Martha said hotly. 'I just think she's

got enough to deal with without having to handle the whole dimensionally transcendental thing.' She gestured around at the control room.

'Hmm. Good point,' he agreed, slipping his long coat back on. 'Come on, then.'

Jenny admitted defeat and walked away from the odd blue shack, back down the alleyway toward the street. Perhaps Mr Vogel in the general store had been mistaken about seeing Martha enter the little outhouse. She resolved to go across to Lapwing's boarding house, in case the Doctor and his companion had followed her advice to take rooms there.

'Jenny!' She turned at the sound of her name to hear a door slam and saw Martha and the tall man approaching. She blinked. Had they both been in there all along, inside such a small accommodation? The shack was a strange thing, faint pearly light illuminating the windows around the top, and the soft glow of the lamp atop it throwing cool colour about the darkening alley. Even with the chill coming in as the sun began to set, there was something strangely warm about the little building.

'Doctor, Martha,' Jenny greeted them with a nod. 'I came looking for you.'

'Something we can help you with, Miss Forrest?' he asked.

The teacher hesitated. She had since learned from Vogel, who fancied himself as the town gossip, of the

Doctor's meeting with Mr Teague and the sheriff, and the rumours abounding from it. People were already talking about the two new arrivals; no one seemed to have seen them ride into town, and Pitt's livery was not caring for any visiting horses. But Jenny had been the subject of similar discussions in the past and, despite the fact that these two were new to her acquaintance, the schoolmarm couldn't shake the undeniable sense that they seemed trustworthy. She sighed. 'It's young Nathan. I am very concerned about his wellbeing. When Martha found him today... I had never before seen him so shaken. I fear a firm hand is exactly *not* what he requires at this moment.'

'Nathan has the dreams,' said the Doctor, rolling the boy's name over his lips. 'Was he the first one to get them? Was he healed first?'

She nodded. 'Right after the Lesters, yes. He took the cure before the rest of the townsfolk.'

'Longest incubation period, maybe?' The Doctor offered the words to Martha.

She nodded back at him. 'How about making a house call, Doctor?'

'Can you show us the way?' the Doctor asked the teacher.

'I don't think that will be possible,' Jenny replied. 'The boy's alone at home. His mother passed away many years ago, you understand. And his father...' She gestured in the direction of the street, where the makeshift festival was still in full swing.

The Doctor shook his head. 'I don't want to talk to his dad. I want to talk to him.'

'But with his father out, we won't be able to enter,' she protested.

'You think?' The tall man eyed her. 'I've learned that I can get into almost anywhere, as long as I have a winning smile and one of these.' He produced a strange ceramic wand from his pocket. Like the shack, it had a blue light that glowed softly. 'Lead on, Miss Forrest.'

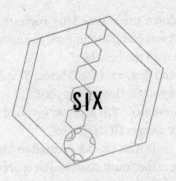

SIX

The Doctor gave the heavy iron lock on the front door a quick *bzzt* from this sonic screwdriver and they were inside. Martha beamed; but the moment they stepped into the rustic dining room-cum-kitchen, her cocky grin faded. The walls of the place were dominated by racks that held a cavalry sword, Apache tomahawks and repeating rifles, even a tiny pocket-sized derringer pistol in a glass case.

'What kind of a person lives in a house like this?' drawled the Doctor, half to himself.

'General Custer?' said Martha. 'I'm detecting a bit of an aggressive motif here.'

Jenny stepped past the orange-yellow embers in the fireplace and called out. 'Nathan? Nathan, are you there? It's Miss Forrest. I'm here with Martha and her friend, the Doctor.'

The boy emerged on the landing above them

and came down the stairs. 'Miss Forrest?' He looked chagrined. 'I was going to come see you in the morning. Apologise for all the fuss, like.'

'Never mind that,' said the Doctor. 'Windows can be fixed easily enough. How about you?'

Nathan hesitated. 'I'm fine, sir. Just had me a turn, that's all. My pa says I'll sleep it off.'

'But can you?' The Doctor crossed to him, taking a careful look at the youth. 'Can you sleep, Nathan?'

He looked away. 'In all honesty, not as well as I'd like.' He sighed. 'My pa, he's not a bad man, you know? He's worried about me but he can't say it outright. Ever since momma passed, he's been lookin' out for me. That's why he got me the cure straight away.'

Martha felt a pang of sympathy for him. 'How old are you?'

'He's 15,' said Jenny.

'Going on 16 this fall!' the youth insisted. 'I ain't no kid, if that's what you're implyin'.'

'Nathan.' The Doctor gave him a steady look. 'These dreams you have, the sickness. Martha and I think there's a connection between them.'

'My pa said I shouldn't talk no more about it.'

'You can talk to us,' Jenny insisted. 'We're here to help you. This man is a doctor, a proper physician, not like that charlatan Godlove.'

'Or close enough,' admitted the Doctor. 'Nathan, if you let me, I might be able to find a way to help you sleep again.'

The boy sighed, and for a moment he seemed like a scared child. 'I'd sure like that.'

They sat opposite each other, the Doctor and the boy, across the kitchen table. Martha sat next to him and opened Nathan's shirt, examining his chest, listening to his heartbeat while the Doctor entered a new setting on his sonic screwdriver.

'What are you looking for?' asked Jenny.

'Scars,' said Martha. 'Lesions or pockmarks, damage to his lungs, anything that could show that he had smallpox. People who survive infection are always marked.' She paused. 'But there's nothing here. He's perfectly healthy, as if he was never sick. It's almost—' Martha gave the Doctor a loaded glance.

'Like he's been regenerated,' he said. The Doctor turned to Nathan and spoke in a soft, kind voice. 'I want you to listen to me,' he told him, waving the sonic back and forth in front of the boy's face, letting the glow of the blue light soothe him. 'Just listen. Concentrate on my voice and the glow, nothing else.'

Nathan gave a sleepy nod.

'Na-ru, na-ru, na-ru,' hummed the Doctor, 'na-ru-na-ru,' The tune was lilting and unearthly, and gradually the boy relaxed. He went slack in the chair, his eyes distant, soothed by the hypnotic mantra.

'What is that peculiar melody?' whispered Jenny.

'Venusian lullaby,' the Doctor said, from the side of his mouth. After a moment, he felt silent and adjusted controls on the device. 'Nathan? How are you feeling?'

'Good,' managed the youth.

'I want you to tell me about the dreams. Tell me what you see.'

'Scared,' Nathan's voice was thick and slow.

'Don't be,' said Martha. 'We're all here. Me and the Doctor and Miss Forrest. There's nothing to be frightened of.'

Jenny gave his hand a squeeze. 'Go on, Nathan. Tell the Doctor what you dreamt.'

Nathan trembled. 'War,' he husked. 'I dream war.'

The way the boy said it sent a chill down Martha's spine. These were not the words of someone with an overactive imagination; somehow, Nathan could really *see* what he was describing.

'A black sky, and it's full of streaks, orange they are, like fire. Iron darts chasin' each other, fast as an eagle. The moon's real big up there, but it ain't right. Too big, too red. A ring around it, shiny.'

'Not Earth,' said the Doctor in a low voice. He traced the sonic screwdriver over Nathan's body as the boy continued.

'The sounds are always the same. Cryin' out, like lost souls. And cannons and lightning, lightning shootin' from the guns. Stone cracking open…'

'Tell us about the creatures,' said Martha. 'The men.'

Nathan shook his head slightly. 'Walk like men, but they ain't men. I seen birds big as steers. Dog-faced things and bundles of thorny sticks that walk an' talk. Monsters like knights outta storybooks, all silver and faceless. Every one of 'em fighting, fighting against the guns. The lightning and the guns.'

The Doctor's eyes narrowed as he studied his device. 'There's an energy trace in him, but very faint. It's only become detectable since he started to dream.'

'Is that a medical instrument of some kind?' asked Jenny.

'It's a lot of things,' Martha replied.

'Nathan, come back now,' said the Doctor, taking the youth's pulse at his neck. 'Wake up.'

The boy blinked and jerked in the chair. 'Whoa. Pa?'

The Doctor shook his head, 'No, your dad's not here right now, but you did great. You were very brave.'

'No,' insisted Nathan, looking past him. 'My pa…'

'He's not here,' repeated Martha; and then she felt the cold metal of a gun barrel press against the back of her skull.

'I beg to differ,' said Sheriff Blaine in a tight, furious voice. He moved out of the shadows from behind her, his face red with anger. 'What in the name of hell do you think you're doing to my son?'

'Ah,' said the Doctor, glancing at Jenny. 'Nathan, as in Nathan Blaine, would that be?'

The teacher gave a weak, sheepish smile. 'Oh yes. I apologise. That detail slipped my mind. I'm so sorry.'

'Not as sorry as I am,' managed Martha, trying very hard not to move.

'Pa, it ain't what you think,' began Nathan, but his father glared at the youth, silencing him.

'Coming home and I saw the light in the kitchen,' he growled, 'and after all that's been and gone I snuck myself in the back way. And lookie here what I find. You again, Doc.' He pulled back the hammer on his pistol. 'You got a breath or two to explain yourself, before I put down this pretty painted cat of yours!'

The Doctor held up his hands. 'Wait, wait! Don't do anything hasty!'

'Hasty, now?' said Blaine. 'Breakin' into a man's property? For that alone I ought to sling you in the jail and let you rot there! And no judge would doubt me fair to put a bullet in you if I chose to!'

'He's trying to help your son, you stupid man!' Jenny shouted suddenly. The normally well-spoken teacher's outburst was a surprise to all of them.

'I don't mean any harm,' said the Doctor.

Martha heard the emotions shifting in the man's voice. 'He's all I got, you understand? I got no family left, nothing but the boy.' She felt the pistol move away. 'He's my responsibility. I promised my wife I'd keep him safe. Do you know what that's like, huh? Being the last one in your family, strugglin' to keep it alive?'

'Yes,' replied the Doctor, with quiet, honest sadness. 'I do.'

Martha turned and saw the look on Blaine's face. His bluster and anger were gone, and he looked sombre and fearful. 'We can help,' she told him. 'But you have to level with us. You must have seen what's going on around here. The sickness and the dreams.'

'It'll pass,' he insisted, but without real conviction. 'It has to.'

'I know what you're trying to do,' said the Doctor, 'you're just trying to keep the townspeople from being afraid. But there's more to this than meets the eye. And I have to get to the bottom of it.'

The white flash came from nowhere, a brilliant blast of actinic light that flared through the windows of the house; a heartbeat later a crashing screech of sound rolled over them, with screams following in its wake.

'Gunfire!' cried Jenny, her hand flying to her mouth.

Blaine shook his head, his face creasing in concern. 'That ain't like no gun I ever heard!' He scrambled towards the door, with Martha, the Doctor and the others following behind.

They came out into the street in time to witness a second blast of light and noise. Streets away, a plume of fire shot into the air, curling up into the evening sky. 'What is that?' said Martha.

'The lightning!' said Nathan. 'The lightning has come!'

Blaine broke into a run, throwing a shout over his shoulder. 'You stay here!'

Martha eyed the fire that was rapidly spreading across a far building. 'Not bloody likely!'

'Then just keep back!' The Doctor pounded after the sheriff.

She followed him, rounding the corner onto Redwater's main street. There were a handful of men, some with pistols and others with rifles, all of them in shocked silence. They had formed a ring around two riders on ragged-looking horses; and Martha's stomach tightened when she caught the horribly familiar sickly sweet scent of seared human flesh. On the wind there was a faint noise, like the buzzing of flies.

There, lying before the horsemen, was a burned body in a smoking heap. She saw the huge pistols in the hands of the mounted riders and had no doubt who had killed the unfortunate soul.

'The guns!' Nathan hissed. 'It's them!'

'Wait, sheriff!' The Doctor grabbed him by the shoulder, but Blaine shrugged him off and kept running. 'Fools rush in!'

Blaine ignored him and confronted the riders, holding his Colt revolver up to aim at them. 'You two! Get outta the saddle right now, before I blow you out!'

Behind him, the Doctor skidded to a halt. His sonic screwdriver was buzzing, signalling him. Quickly, he drew out the device and twisted the control settings on its ceramic collar.

For the first time, the lawman got a good look at the two men and his eyes widened. 'Can't be… It's not right.'

'You know them?' asked the Doctor.

Blaine frowned. 'Hank Kutter and Will "Tangleleg" Bly… Had wanted posters up for 'em in my office for months now. But the word came down from the

Marshal's office on the telegraph. They're both dead… The roadhouse they were hidin' out in burned to the ground. Not a stick of it left!'

'It would seem otherwise,' said the Doctor. 'Sheriff, I don't think they're what they seem…'

Blaine stepped away. 'With all due respect, Doc, I'm the law in these parts, and I'll deal with trouble my way!' He advanced on the riders. 'Last chance!' he yelled. 'Step down or else!'

The longriders exchanged a cold look, and then did as they were told. Kutter and Tangleleg ran their gaze over everyone in the street, townsfolk and armed men, women and children alike. The Doctor was certain that they lingered for a moment on him, on Martha and on the boy Nathan.

'These highbinders been shooting up the place, sheriff!' Loomis Teague called out, staring down a Winchester rifle at the two outlaws. He pointed the barrel of the gun at the smouldering corpse. 'Killed Fess Logan like a dog in the street… Burned him, they did!'

'Burned,' repeated the Doctor.

'You just earned yourselves a necktie party, boys,' growled Blaine. 'Now you can drop them there hoglegs and go quiet, or else take a bellyful of lead!'

The longriders made no sound, gave no sign they had even heard what the lawman said.

A few feet away, Martha and Jenny stood in the shadow of the general store's awning, with Nathan between them. 'I've never seen faces so pallid before,' said the schoolteacher in a hushed whisper. 'They're so pale and sickly looking… If you saw a man like that by the side of the road, you'd think him a corpse!'

'Maybe that's what they are,' Nathan murmured.

The Doctor glanced at his sonic screwdriver, distracted for a moment. 'The same reading… But it's *older*, somehow.'

Kutter turned his head to face Blaine and spoke. 'Where is the healer?' We know he was here. Where is he?'

'The Doc?' The sheriff shot a glance at the Doctor.

'The healer,' repeated Tangleleg. 'Tell us where he is, or this won't be the end to it.' He gave a languid nod towards the dead body and the burning building.

'He's talking about Godlove,' hissed Martha. 'They're after him!'

The sheriff's fury was at its fullest. 'I don't know who or what you think you are, but I'm done talking.' His gun came up.

'Blaine, *don't*!' The Doctor called out a warning, but he was ignored. The lawman fired, and Teague and all the other men with guns did the same.

But Kutter and Tangleleg didn't fall; they turned into blurs. Too fast for the eye to catch them, the longriders dodged out of the path of the gunfire. Some rounds seemed to rip into them, but they did nothing but spin them about. Blaine fanned the hammer on his Colt, but every shot he fired hissed through empty air.

And then the outlaws paid them back. Kutter flashed

forward, striking down Teague with the butt of his heavy pistol, knocking him to the floor. Tangleleg lashed out with punches and the men who they connected with went flying, as if they'd been hit by a colossal impact. It all happened so fast, in instants.

'Martha, look out!' The Doctor's cry came a second too late. Kutter slammed her aside and shoved Jenny away, coming to a sudden halt with his pistol at Nathan's head.

'No!' shouted the lawman. 'He's just a boy!'

Martha got slowly to her feet, feeling the tension in her ribs from a spreading bruise. She saw the Doctor standing with Blaine in the middle of the dirt street, both men trying to keep the two longriders in their sight.

'Stop this.' The Doctor's voice was level and firm, a great anger boiling away underneath his steady, iron-hard gaze. 'I am asking you to stop this before it goes any further.'

Kutter studied him, his expression never changing. 'The question remains. Where is the healer? You will tell me, or I kill the young one. Then these females.'

'And then everyone in this settlement,' added Tangleleg. 'Until we have an answer. We will spare them if you answer.'

'Papa?' Nathan's eyes pleaded with his father.

Finally, Blaine spat and glared at the townsfolk. 'Put your guns down. Now!' He tossed his pistol to the dirt and the others grudgingly followed suit. 'OK,' said the sheriff, holding up his hands. 'I'll tell you, just don't hurt the boy. Godlove and his redskin, they rode out to the south, toward Dekkerville. That's where he was headin'… Now just let my son go.'

Martha saw the shift in the Doctor's expression. She saw the look in his eyes and suddenly she *knew* what he'd seen. 'They're lying!' The longriders had no intention of keeping their promise.

Kutter reacted, shoving Nathan aside. The massive pistol in his grip turned to face Blaine and it discharged with a thunderous shriek. A bolt of blazing white energy leapt from the muzzle and speared the lawman through the middle of his chest, killing him instantly.

Nathan screamed, his voice rising into the chorus of yells and cries from the rest of the townsfolk as Tangleleg fired wildly into the buildings, seeding chaos and fire.

'Why?' bellowed the Doctor, as the boy rushed to his father's side with Jenny at his heels. 'Why did you do that?' He snarled, his eyes flashing with towering rage, advancing towards the outlaw.

Kutter studied him. 'You're different,' he noted. 'Unlike.'

The Doctor's was furious. 'He told you what you wanted to know! You didn't have to kill him!'

For a long second Kutter held the gun towards the Doctor, and Martha gasped, terrified the longrider would shoot him down as well. 'He would have come after us,' the gunman said, in a flat, matter-of-fact voice.

'Examples must be made.'

The pistol dipped, the aim falling toward Nathan.

'No!' The Doctor threw up his hands.

Martha saw it happen. She felt the sickening lurch in the pit of her stomach as the weapon fired. The bolt struck out, dazzling her.

Jenny saw it too; and she threw herself at the boy, forcing him to the dirt as Kutter pulled the trigger. The shot went wide, missing the boy and striking the teacher.

The woman's scream filled the night air as the blast of energy tore into her.

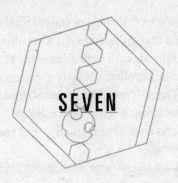

SEVEN

The TARDIS doors slammed open and the Doctor raced inside with Jenny's unconscious body in his arms.

Martha came in, pulling the doors shut behind her. In the confusion and chaos following the gunfight, it had been easy to slip away down the alley; she felt terrible leaving poor Nathan out there, with only his father's corpse for company, but the sheriff was beyond her help. Jenny Forrest, on the other hand, was still clinging to life, and Martha had a duty to do whatever she could to save her.

'Get the medical kit, white box with a green crescent moon on it,' snapped the Doctor, laying the teacher down gently on the gridded decking of the control room. 'Quick, quick, *quick*!'

Martha raced across the chamber and found the medical kit sitting on top of a woman's jacket. Inside the plastic box were dozens of vials of fluid and a green, jelly-like pod that pulsated as if it were alive.

She brought the case to their patient. 'How is she?'

The Doctor unrolled a length of burnt, fragmented material off Jenny's shoulder to reveal the damage from Kutter's gun. It had been a glancing shot – a direct hit would have taken her life instantly – but the injury was still very serious.

'It looks as if she was struck by lightning,' said Martha.

'That was a phased energy weapon. Coherent plasma matrix suspended in a particle beam.' He handed her an injector. 'Here. The red and blue vials, full dose, into her carotid artery.'

'Yes, Doctor,' she replied, and did as he directed. Martha's eyes were drawn to Jenny's face; her skin was drained of colour and thin lines of grey were creeping out from the place where she'd been hit. 'What is that?'

'Decay stream,' he snapped. 'Like the venom on a poisoned blade. If the wound doesn't kill you, the toxic aftershock will.'

Jenny groaned and Martha felt a flicker of life fading beneath her fingertips. 'Her pulse is slowing. Oh no, I think we're going to lose her.'

'Not today.' The Doctor snapped his fingers at her. 'Give me the green squishy thing, it's a medical nanogene pod!' She handed him the slimy knot of jelly and he pulled an activating rip-tab, then pressed it into place against Jenny's skin. The pod dissolved into her flesh in a glitter of light, but it didn't seem to work. The woman's back arched and she went slack.

'We're too late!' snarled the Doctor. 'She's crashing!'

Martha shook her head. 'Like you said, not today.' She bent down over the prone woman and put her hands over Jenny's chest, pumping a one-two-three rhythm to keep the teacher's heart beating. For long moments, nothing seemed to happen; and then a rattling gasp issued out of the woman's mouth and the grey threads began to fade away.

The Doctor threw her a weary smile. 'Martha Jones. Lifesaver.'

'Team effort,' she replied; but she found she couldn't smile back. 'Only this one, though. What about the others?'

'Don't keep score, you'll only make yourself feel worse. We just help the ones we can.' He gathered up Jenny and Martha helped him carry her to the wide, threadbare chair next to the central console.

Jenny dozed and Martha studied her, watching the nanogenes do their amazing work. 'It's like watching a fast-forward movie. I can actually see the tissue healing.'

'They're tiny robots,' the Doctor explained, 'half-organic and half-machine, not much larger than a few atoms in size. Programmed to repair diseased tissue and dismantle germs. They'll have a near-fatal injury healed up in a few weeks.'

'Where did you get them?' she asked. 'It's not Earth stuff.'

'It's New Earth stuff, actually,' he said. 'I borrowed the kit when I was there with Rose, a while back. That was the last of it, though.'

'Oh. I thought the logo looked familiar.' She glanced at the discarded jacket. 'And I did wonder who that belonged to.'

The Doctor looked away. 'Jenny will be OK. If we hadn't got her into the TARDIS in time…' He trailed off, his thoughts turning inward.

'Those nanogenes, do you think that guy Godlove got his hands on some of them? Is that what cured the smallpox?'

He shook his head. 'Nanomachines die off once their job is done, but traces of them linger in your system for months. I didn't detect anything like that in Nathan's bloodstream. No, he was cured by something else, some sort of bio-energy engram. Totally different technology.' The Doctor walked in a slow circle. 'And those two men. They had a similar energy trace about them.'

'Godlove, the cure, those maniacs with those guns. You're sure there's a connection between all three?'

'There's no doubt in my mind. I just wish I knew what it was.'

'But who were they?'

He sat heavily. 'Kutter and Tangleleg, Blaine called them. Outlaws. But I've never seen low-life cowboys using directed energy weapons instead of six-guns, have you?'

'Advanced technology,' Martha sounded it out. 'Something from another planet or time period, then?'

The Doctor gave a slow, solemn nod. 'At first I thought we'd stumbled on something local – weird and strange, but local – only now I'm not so sure.' He pointed at the air with his finger. 'We can't let this go unchecked, Martha. There's something alien running free out there in the Wild West, and we have to find it. Find it and *stop it*.'

'Then we have to track down this Alvin Godlove. He's the key to it all. We need to learn his secret.' She frowned. 'But how do we find him before those two psychos do? You saw what they did, they don't care about who they hurt or what they destroy. Who knows how many other people they've killed just to get here?'

'Dekkerville, Blaine said.' The Doctor's hands hovered over the controls of the TARDIS. 'It's tricky, but we could try a sideways shunt in space with the same temporal coordinates.'

Martha's frown deepened. 'No offence, but we might draw a lot of attention if you materialise a police box in the middle of town square.'

He nodded again. 'You could be right. Kutter said I was different. I think he might have been able to sense who I am, just a little. And if there's aliens involved, they might spot a moving time capsule like a flare on a dark night.'

'We'll find another way to get to Dekkerville, then.'

'No,' said a weak voice. They both turned and found Jenny reaching up from the chair. 'That's… wrong…'

Martha knelt beside her. 'Don't try to talk. Just rest. You'll be fine, I promise, but you have to rest.'

Jenny shook her head. 'No, listen to me…' She coughed. 'I heard you. Dekkerville… That was a lie. Blaine lied to those men… Godlove… Didn't go south. *North.* He went northwards.'

'Well, well. Clever sheriff,' said the Doctor. 'He sent them on a wild goose chase.'

'So where is Alvin Godlove's medicine show now, then?' asked Martha.

'Ironhill,' husked the woman.

A sudden, warm tightness at her shoulder sent small thrills of pain down Jenny's arm and she hissed, clutching at it. The schoolteacher had woken up in her own bed, rolled the bedclothes off and sat up, peering into the morning light that filtered through her window. Her first thoughts were that the whole frightful experience had been a night terror of her own.

Now, she gingerly pulled her nightgown an inch down her arm to reveal the site of the pain. A poultice was secured in place there with a bandage, and the skin either side was tender and livid, as if she had been too long in the sun. Jenny's mouth was dry and she took a sip of water from the glass on her nightstand.

In fits and starts, pieces of the night before returned

to her. Taking the Doctor and Martha to see young Nathan; the boy's peculiar stories, told to them in his mournful trance; and then the horror of the longriders in the main street.

A gasp escaped her lips. The memory of incredible, heart-stopping pain flooded through her and for a moment she felt it again. The wash of murderous heat as the white flash of light struck her. The agony, greater than anything she had ever experienced before, smashing her into a dark, rumbling blackness. *She had been shot. She should have been dead.*

Jenny struggled out of bed and doggedly dressed herself, her face twisting in frustration as she attempted to remember. 'There was a room,' she said aloud, 'the walls honey-yellow and warm, like beaten gold.' A domed space, or so it had seemed, with a strange device at the centre. A thing of brass and crystal, delicate and yet powerful. Something about it made her think of an engine, but she could not fathom why. 'But where?' she asked herself. She knew Redwater, having lived there for these past five years, and she knew full well that no building such as the one she had been in existed there.

'The Doctor.' She remembered him carrying her, carrying her towards the blue box. He had been talking to her all the way, whispering. Telling her to hold on, to stay awake. 'And Martha.' Jenny recalled the girl's face with perfect clarity, hovering close to her, breathing life back into her lungs. There was something else, as well, something on the tip her tongue. She'd told them...

Told them what?

A delicate knock sounded at the door, and Mrs Toomey entered with a tray of breakfast things. The elderly woman gawked at her. 'Good grief, Miss Forrest, but you shouldn't ought to be up and about! You took a dreadful injury! You were dead to the world when that young Doctor fella brought you back here!'

She shook her head. 'Thank you kindly for your concern, but I feel well enough to be about the day.' She glanced out of the window and frowned, the light of the morning showing the blackened ruins among the undamaged buildings, where before stores and homes had stood. 'I must speak with him.'

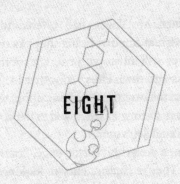

EIGHT

'All I'm sayin' is,' Loomis Teague grated, 'how do we know that pair o' hellhounds ain't gonna come riding back here looking for some payback, once they figure they been gulled by Blaine?'

He looked across the room to the Doctor, and Martha hid a small smile. A day ago, Teague had been ready to turn a knife on the Doctor and fleece him; but now Teague and the rest of the townsfolk in Redwater were looking to him for guidance, even if they weren't aware of it themselves. He had that way about him, she mused. He was take-charge, he always had an answer. In chaos, he became the eye of the storm.

'They won't be back,' said the Doctor. 'You deal with as many troublemakers and all-around nasty folks as I have, and after a while you learn to read them.' He walked slowly around the table in the middle of the store, giving everyone in the room a steady look.

The owner, Mr Vogel, had offered to host this 'meeting of great import' in his shop, as that was the only building still intact with enough room for all the storeowners and town elders to gather in. Their usual haunt across the way, the Bluebird saloon, was a burnt-out shadow of its former self, razed to the dirt by a stray shot from Tangleleg's gun.

'Those men aren't out for revenge, Loomis. I know their kind. They're *hunters*. They're looking for a very specific prey. They won't come back because there's nothing here for them. No targets.'

'Bounty riders, you mean?' asked Vogel. 'Regulators sent by some dark agency to find Professor Godlove? But to what end?'

'That's what we're going to find out,' said Martha. The men seemed a bit uncomfortable with a woman taking part in town business, but she had no time for their delicate sensibilities. 'We're going to have a very serious chat with our friend Alvin.'

Zachariah Hawkes, who had been chewing his lower lip with greater and greater impatience, finally stepped forward and flapped his hands. 'With all due respect to the little filly here, I have to say that my concerns lie not with our neighbours in Ironhill or parts beyond, but with the good folks in our community!' A ripple of agreement passed through the assembled men. Hawkes gestured at the air. 'With the sudden and most untimely passing of our steadfast Sheriff Tobias Blaine, Redwater finds itself without the rule of law and at the mercy of future attacks!' He produced a smudged copy of the *Chronicle*, with a smeared headline that read *Town Attacked! Hooligans on the Prowyl!* 'I have already produced a new edition saying as much in my editorial!'

'You spelt "prowl" wrong,' offered Martha.

The Doctor took the paper off him, gave it a grim onceover, and then screwed it into a ball. 'I've never liked sensationalist tabloids,' he said firmly, thrusting the ball of paper back into Hawkes's inky hands. 'You people need to pull together, not panic and jump at shadows!'

'Sir, you are correct,' said Joe Pitt, kneading his hat brim. 'And I think, we was all mightily awed of how you stood up to those snakes and then looked to Miss Forrest. Clearly you're a man of courage and learning, and I'd hasten to say, we could do no better than ask you to fill Tobias's boots for the duration.' He held out a hand, and in it was a six-pointed tin star. 'I'd like to propose the Doctor for the job of Town Sheriff.'

'Seconded!' said Vogel, pressing the badge into the Doctor's grip.

The Doctor's firm expression slipped in a moment of genuine surprise. 'Whoa, whoa, *whoa*! Oh no,' he shook his head. 'I wore one of these once, ages ago, and all it got me was trouble. I'm not doing *that* again.'

Martha saw Jenny enter the store, the menfolk bowing and making space for her. 'You all right?'

'Thanks to you both,' nodded the teacher. 'I owe you my life.'

Martha felt slightly abashed. 'Ah, it's OK. That's what we do, me and him. It's our thing.'

'Doctor, please,' Joe was saying. 'We're all at sea here. What took place last night… Well, we ain't never seen the like.'

'All the more reason to *pull together*,' repeated the Doctor. 'I've got to find Alvin Godlove, or else other towns, other people will suffer like you did last night. Tobias Blaine, Fess Logan and everyone else who was hurt, they're just the start. Whether he knows it or not, Godlove's leaving a trail of death and pain in his wake and I have to stop it.' He approached Teague. 'Loomis,' he said sternly, 'Listen to me. It's time you grew up, my old mucker. Put away the cards and the poker chips, get rid of that knife, stop going down the pub every night with your mates and getting into fights. This is your town, and you need to do right by it. Take some responsibility.'

Teague gave a nervous nod. 'O-OK, Doc. Whatever you say. I guess I have been a mite selfish in recent times. Guess I could do better…'

'I know you will.' The Doctor patted him on the chest and when he took his hand away, the tin star was pinned on the man's waistcoat. 'Sheriff Teague here is going to do the right thing, isn't that so?'

Teague gawked at the badge. 'Sheriff?' Then the idea bedded in with him, and suddenly the gambler drew himself up, straight, steady and clear-eyed. '*Yeah. That I am.*' Teague nodded toward Pitt. 'And the first order of business is, get the Doctor and Miss Martha here some horses. They got business in Ironhill.'

'You're riding out, then?' asked Jenny.

'We have to,' said Martha.

'That mining town's two days from here on horseback,' said Hawkes. 'Godlove's liable to be gone before you get there!'

'That's if they follow the stagecoach trail. There's a shortcut through the hills,' offered Pitt. 'Take it at a gallop and with the wind at your back, you'll make it before sunset.'

'Rough land out there,' noted Teague. 'Nothing but rocks and rattlers. You get lost in the hills, the coyotes'll be chewin' on your bones by nightfall.'

'I know of a body, knows the route,' Joe continued. 'Reckon he might throw in as your guide, like.'

'I've still got a fair bit of winnings left over from yesterday,' said the Doctor. 'Use that to pay for everything, and keep the change.'

The stableman nodded and headed off as the meeting began to break up. Loomis Teague led the men out, giving out orders in a strong, commanding voice.

'Who would have thought a card-sharp and a reprobate would have it in him to be a town official?' Jenny asked lightly, watching him go.

'I've got an eye for people,' said the Doctor. 'Sometimes, all a person needs is a little trust to put them on the straight and narrow.'

Jenny took his hand. 'Thank you, Doctor. If you

hadn't been here last night, then this whole town would be cinders.'

He eyed her. 'I'm not the one who saved Nathan's life, Jenny. *You're* the one who pushed him out of the path of that beam. You saved him.'

'I did what I thought was right,'

Martha studied her bandages. 'How's the shoulder?'

'Painful,' Jenny admitted, 'but much preferable to the other option.' She looked away. 'I don't know what you did, but I know it should not have healed this quickly. Are you using Godlove's medicine? Will I have the dreams?'

'Not unless you eat loads of cheese before you go to bed,' said the Doctor. 'Don't be afraid. We just used a cure… something that's a bit before its time. You know, like Captain Nemo's submarine in *Twenty Thousand Leagues* or the rocket in *From the Earth to the Moon.*'

'A science of the future?' Jenny replied. 'How marvellous.'

Vogel approached with a pile of gear and dropped it on the table before them. 'Doctor, Miss Jones. Please, take these as a gift.'

Martha reached out and took a hat from the pile. 'Ooh, cool!' She sat it on her head at a jaunty angle. 'Very Madonna, don't you think?' She fingered a poncho and frowned. 'Not that, though. It's too *Ugly Betty* for me.'

'Oh, I quite like the *Man-With-No-Name* look,' said the Doctor.

'Well, you would,' she sniffed.

He chose a hat, then picked up a thick leather holster and belt, and cinched it in place around his waist. 'That's snug.'

Vogel smiled. 'I'll hazard you'll want this as well.' The storekeeper slid a black revolver across the table toward him.

'Colt model of 1873, single-action .45 calibre pistol,' said the Doctor, eyeing the gun coldly. 'Commonly known as the Peacemaker. They called it "the Gun that Won the West"… The pistol behind a million gunfights, range wars and shootouts.' He shook his head. 'You can keep it.'

Vogel's smile slipped. 'But Doctor, surely you won't venture out into the wilds without a firearm? This, sir, is the finest gun ever made, an invaluable tool to any man. In these days, it is as necessary to have as the clothes on your back!'

'A weapon is only a tool,' said the Doctor carefully. 'I've heard a lot of people say that over the years. But so is a hammer, and if that's the only tool you have, pretty soon everything starts to look like a nail.' He pushed the revolver back toward Vogel. 'No thanks.'

'Then why did you take the gun belt?' asked the storekeeper.

The Doctor gave him an *isn't it obvious?* look. 'For this.' With a flourish, he pulled out his sonic screwdriver, twirled the device around his fingers and slipped it into the holster. 'There. Perfect!'

* * *

Joe had a trio of chestnut mares waiting for them at the livery stable, and Martha grinned widely. She'd not ridden a horse since the Doctor had taken her to the Lake District, but this would be very different to that ride through the English countryside. She was looking forward to galloping across the dusty range at full tilt. But the Doctor's expression turned stormy when he saw the face of their trail guide.

'Nathan,' he said, in a blunt tone. 'What are you doing here?'

The boy sat tall in the saddle, putting on an outward show of strength. Still, Martha saw where his eyes were puffy from where he had been crying. 'Doc,' he replied. 'Joe told me you need someone to take you to Ironhill.'

The Doctor glared at the stableman. 'Find someone else.'

But Nathan shook his head. 'That'll be a long wait for a train that don't come, Doc,' he insisted. 'Fact of the matter is, everyone in town is afraid to leave.'

'Boy's right,' said Joe. 'No one wants to ride out while those two demons are still around.'

'They're not demons,' growled the Doctor. 'I've seen demons, and they're not them.' He strode over to Nathan's mount. 'Do you really know the shortcut?'

'Yes.'

'Why do you want to come to Ironhill with us? Don't lie to me, Nathan. I'll know it if you do.'

The boy swallowed back emotion, and glanced at Martha and Jenny, his eyes shimmering. 'I want justice for my pa. I want to make sure no one else gets hurt like he did.'

'So do I.' The Doctor reached up and pulled out a pistol hidden in Nathan's belt. 'But *this* is not how we do it. You understand me? Cos if you think different, you can get off that horse right now and go…' He paused, failing to find the right words. '… drink your milk.'

After a moment, the boy nodded. 'Yes, sir.'

He handed the pistol to Joe. 'Give that to Loomis to look after.'

'Good luck and Godspeed,' said Jenny.

With a swift motion, the Doctor swung up into the saddle and took his mount's reins. 'Right then,' he said, smiling slightly as Martha worked her way carefully onto her horse. 'Ready?'

Martha nodded. 'Ready!'

The Doctor filled his lungs with a deep breath and tipped a finger to his hat. 'Let's ride!' he called, with obvious glee, cracking the reins. '*Yah!*'

With a thunder of hooves, the horses raced away into the wilderness, dust trailing into the air behind them.

NINE

Alvin Godlove held up his hands and grinned widely, his pearly teeth shining. 'Ladies and gentlemen, please, please! One at a time!' He flashed his winning smile back and forth. Alvin's teeth were one of the best things about him, his momma had always said, and he made sure he kept them gleaming. Something about his smile made the dumb rubes in these hick dirt-farmer towns come over all trusting, and that was just what he wanted. Many a time had Alvin used his cheeky grin to win over the hearts of communities just like this one – what was it called again? Iron-Swill? Iron-Pill? – and open their pockets too.

Of course, now he didn't actually have to *lie* about his amazing medical abilities. Not like before, when he was mixing up batches of rot-gut whiskey with sulphur and sugar, and calling it a remedy.

Now he had the cure-all. He had, if it wasn't too

pompous to think it, the power of life and death in his very hands.

And the cashy money was rolling in. Behind him, Walking Crow followed with his perpetually morose expression, dolefully taking the offers of coins and paper dollars, even family jewels and other rarities. Heck, back on the medicine show's box wagon, they even had an oil painting that some rancher had traded for a little of Alvin's tender care.

He halted at the steps to the old woman's house and held up his hands again. 'Please! Good people, there is but only one of me and I can move only so fast to do my works.' Godlove looked out and saw desperate faces, all of them turned to him, pleading and imploring. The little mining town was crying out for help; the smallpox had come and ripped through their populace like a tornado, and those that weren't already newly interred in the bone orchard with the rest of the deaders, were either dying in the sick tent off main street or perishing by inches in their own homes. This place was perfect. Already a lot of folks were back up and walking around, thank to his ministrations, and in a day or so the old biddy who lived here would be joining them… Provided, of course, that she could cross his palm with silver. Or gold. Or whatever valuables she had to give.

'Allow me to do what I can for the poor lady…' He glanced at Walking Crow, unable to remember the name.

'Weems,' whispered the Pawnee.

'Mrs Weems!' Alvin smiled wider. 'I must attend to her!'

Inside the house, Godlove once again allowed Walking Crow to deal with the business of the payment from the old lady's son while he climbed the stairs to the bedroom. Entering, he fought down the urge to choke. The air inside the room was foul with sweat and that nasty old-people funk. A frail thing, more a bag of skin full of bones, lay on the bed.

'Hello?' said a reedy voice. 'Are you the doctor?'

He bowed. 'Professor Alvin Q. Godlove at your service, ma'am. I am here to rid you of the vile smallpox.'

She pointed feebly to a brown bottle on the nightstand. 'I've been taking your potion, but it's done me no good.' Alvin came closer and saw the now-familiar scarring of smallpox lesions on her aged face.

'Don't you worry none,' he soothed, in his best Southern Gentleman accent. 'I'm going to administer a proper treatment, now that you've made a suitable donation.' Godlove reached inside his jacket and drew out something that resembled a handgun. He gasped as he touched it; out of sight, tiny needles nipped at the flesh of his palm where he held it, and the skin seemed to merge into the strange organic metal of the device.

'Oh my!' gasped the woman. 'Is that a pistol? Are you going to put me out of my misery like some lame mule?'

'Nothing of the sort.' Alvin shook his head, twisting

a dial on the side of the device. Usually they didn't talk back to him when he was working. Most of the time, they were too out of it to even know there was another person in the room, and he made sure that he had his privacy. 'Doctor-patient confidentiality,' he would say.

The lengthy barrel shifted and retracted, revealing a glowing green nodule. His breath came in short gasps, as it always did when he used the cure-all. 'You just hush up now.' He aimed it at her body and squeezed the trigger; at once a fan of emerald light washed out and engulfed her. The old woman moaned, and slipped into unconsciousness. Gradually, the pockmarks and scars across her flesh became faint and faded, as something approximating a normal tone returned to her skin.

Walking Crow found him on the back stoop of the house after he was done. Alvin was panting and sweating.

The Pawnee folded his arms. 'It's getting harder, isn't it?'

Godlove got up abruptly and stalked away. 'What the hell are you talkin' about?'

'I watch you,' he said, following him back toward the wagon. 'I see you.' He pointed to where Alvin had his hand clenched tight. 'It is like a wild beast. You may think you have tamed it, but you have not. It bites you and draws blood.'

Godlove glanced down at his hand. Where he had held the cure-all there were whorls and circles writhing in his palm, dots where tiny wires like the spines of a cactus had implanted themselves in his living flesh. There were moments when he felt the thing working at him, shifting the bones and meat of his hand; and lately he was feeling it in his arm and shoulder too. His hand contracted into a ball. 'I know what I'm doing,' he retorted. 'In case you hadn't noticed, we're richer than we've ever been! This thing—' He tapped the pocket where the device rested. 'This thing is the greatest boon a man could ever have!'

Walking Crow shook his head slowly. 'I have touched it too. I heard the voice inside it. It is hungry. All you have done is make that hunger strong.' He looked away. 'The thing is a curse. We should kill it.'

Godlove snorted with harsh laughter. 'No wonder you people couldn't hold on to this land! You got no guts!' He prodded the Pawnee in the chest. 'This "thing" will make me wealthy, you'll see! You don't like it, you can go back to that rat hole where I found you!'

The Pawnee turned away. 'It feeds on decay,' he said quietly. 'What can anything that feasts on death be but bad medicine?'

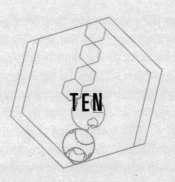

TEN

At first it wasn't fun at all; as Martha Jones clung to her horse with one hand, using the other to keep her hat pressed to her head so it wouldn't fly off, riding felt very far away from fun *indeed*.

Nathan was as good as his word, taking them on a winding course through the foothills, and within a short time they were racing through narrow canyons and arroyos, riding like the wind.

The Doctor kept pace with her, eagerly urging his mount on and grinning wildly. His coat crackled and flapped out behind him like a cloak. 'This is great, isn't it?' he thrilled, and he let out a *yee-hah* rebel yell at the top of his lungs. That was the Doctor, he could make a good time out of anything, never mind if it was terrifying as well.

Martha managed a faint smile, but concentrated more on staying in the saddle. This wasn't some gentle canter about the countryside; they were going full tilt here, at *Pony Express* speeds. But little by little, Martha got into the swing of it. The slightly brittle smile on her face began to widen and, by the time they had crested the hills and started down the other side toward a distant smudge of buildings, she was starting to let herself enjoy it. It was a bit scary to be on the back of a wilful animal galloping along at breakneck pace, but the thrill of it gradually tipped the balance against the fear. Martha dared to sit taller in the saddle, and soon she felt like she had the measure of it.

'Easy,' she said to herself. 'A walk in the park. Uh, desert.'

Joe had picked a swift but even-tempered horse for her, and she felt a bit bad about forgetting to ask its name. She shot the Doctor a sly look that he missed completely and bent down to whisper in the animal's ear. 'I know. I'll call you Rose, how about that?' She grinned to herself. Growing up, Martha hadn't been one of those girls who adored books like *Black Beauty*, gymkhanas and that kind of thing. Living on the outskirts of London's sprawl, all that horsy countryside stuff had seemed a million miles away from the world she came from; but now, she was starting to see the appeal of it.

With her panic fading, Martha took in some of the landscape as it flashed by. The rusty earth ranged away toward the distant horizon beneath a brilliant cobalt-coloured sky dappled with thin streaks of cloud. Buttes

– great flat-topped mountains with sheer, rippled sides
– reached up towards the blue. From a distance they
resembled gigantic anthills, the vast pedestals carved
from the living rock by wind and erosion. This was the
beating heart of the American Frontier, the West in all
its vibrant glory. It struck Martha how lucky she was
to be able to see it like this; how many people could
say they had seen this country when it was still a blank
page, with history being written upon it?

The ground flattened out and the trail became better
defined. Martha had to admit that Nathan seemed to
know his stuff. Even if she'd been walking, there was
no way she would have spotted the shortcut through
the hills, let alone guide mounted riders along it. It had
taken them the best part of a day, with a couple of stops
for shade and water, but he'd got them to Ironhill just as
he promised. The only thing that bothered her was the
teenager's grim, morose expression.

She knew shock when she saw it; Martha had seen
the same thing at the Royal Hope, when a doctor broke
the news to someone that a loved one had died. Denial,
refusal to believe the truth, anger. She could see all those
emotions churning away behind Nathan's haunted eyes.
The boy would never have admitted it, but he was very
fragile right now. It hadn't even been a day since he lost
his father, and he was hiding his bereavement behind a
wall of anger; but she also knew that she couldn't force
him. *He'll have to grieve in his own time, in his own way*, she
thought to herself.

They slowed to a gentle trot as they approached the edge of town. A battered sign reading 'Welcome To Ironhill' arched over the main road. Faces turned to study them as they came closer.

At first glance, Ironhill didn't seem a lot different to Redwater; the same kind of clapboard buildings, a dirt main street, wagons here and there and horses at hitching posts. But then Martha saw the grubby white sick tent isolated off at the far side of town; and then she took a good look at the people.

They had arrived at Redwater and found a town united in celebration after the defeat of an epidemic. Ironhill, on the other hand, was still reeling from the passing of the disease. Hollow-eyed, grim faces looked up at them from street corners and out of windows. The town had a derelict, ruined feel to it.

The scent of decay hung in the air along with the stringent chemical smell of harsh soap. Many buildings had been hastily boarded up, or they had makeshift red banners hanging outside in the limp breeze, marking the places where infection had been found.

She heard Nathan gasp. 'Mother of mercy. They must've had it a lot worse than back home.'

The Doctor grimaced as they passed the undertakers, spotting a dead body in a casket as the lid was being nailed down. 'It's smallpox all right. That poor bloke had the scars on his face.'

They halted at the livery stable. Martha threw a nod towards the main street. 'It's weird, though. If this place was hit by an outbreak, then you'd think people would be keeping to themselves, staying indoors.' Wherever she looked, townsfolk were still coming and going. She could even hear the mangled notes of a poorly played piano wafting out from a saloon toward the other end of town.

'Maybe that'd be true back East,' said Nathan, 'but out here folks don't like to admit they might be licked by something they can't see.'

The Doctor nodded in agreement. 'People always try to put a brave face on things, no matter how bad it gets.' Nathan didn't see the Doctor glance at him and then to Martha.

'So what next?' she asked.

He dismounted with a twirl of his coat. 'Nathan, if you would be so kind as to hitch up the horses. And then we'll go see a man about a cure.'

Martha made a move to climb out of the saddle and then paused. 'Now, how do I get down and still look ladylike?'

Nathan shook his head with a faint smirk. 'City folk. Huh.' He offered her his hand. 'Let me help you, Miss Martha.'

'Howdy!' The Doctor tipped his hat and smiled. 'I do *love* this hat, you know. It's a very fine hat indeed.'

The stableman, a bald, stocky chap in a stained leather apron, gave the Doctor an up-and-down look. 'You're not familiar to me,' he noted.

'No?' he replied. 'Well, don't let that worry you. I'm very nice once you get acquainted with me. What's that old saying? Strangers are just friends you don't know yet.'

'You're drawin' attention, that's for sure,' said the man.

He was right; nearby, the Doctor saw a few thin children, a wary-looking Pawnee and a chubby washerwoman studying the new arrivals.

'I so often do,' he agreed.

'I don't mean to seem inhospitable, but it's my estimation you might be best off getting back in the saddle and riding on.' The stableman frowned.

'And why might that be?'

The man gestured around. 'Ironhill's shaking off a sickness. Town ain't in no state for whatever kind of business you'll have.'

'We ain't here for work,' Nathan said curtly. 'We're here to find a—'

'A friend.' The Doctor quickly spoke over him. 'Well, more of a passing acquaintance really. I suppose you could call him a fellow academic, if you used the term loosely.'

'*Very* loosely,' murmured Martha.

'You're talking about the Professor?' The stableman's expression changed. 'Why didn't you say? The man's brought a ray o' light to this godforsaken place, and that's a fact!' He grinned. 'Last I heard, he was doing his good works over at the Widow Weems's place. He's made a lot of folks better with that potion of his. We're mighty grateful.'

'No one's had the nightmares yet, then?' said the boy. 'The bad dreams?'

'The what?' The bald man's brow furrowed.

'Nothing,' said the Doctor. 'You were saying?'

The stableman thought for a moment. 'His wagon's parked over yonder.' He pointed. 'In the street behind the bakery.'

'But where's Godlove?' Nathan's voice was almost a snarl, and his hands tightened into fists.

Martha shot the Doctor a warning look.

'Can't say for sure where he is now,' answered the stableman.

The Doctor pushed back his hat with a finger. 'Martha, why don't you and Nathan have a look at Professor Godlove's wagon, see if he's about?'

She nodded, catching the unspoken addendum in the Doctor's look that said *And stay out of trouble!* 'Gotcha. What are you going to do?'

'I think I'll take a stroll down main street, see if I can't look up our good pal Alvin.'

The music inside the saloon was feeble, but it was mildly entertaining. The few patrons at the bar were largely quiet, leaving the tables to the man of the hour.

Three of them, a group of roughneck brothers and apparent ne'er-do-wells, hoisted their glasses in salute. 'Here's to you, sir,' said the tallest of the trio. 'Anythin' we can do to repay you for all you did, you just say the word!'

Alvin Godlove saluted back. 'Thank you, gentlemen.' He smirked. 'You see, my dear,' he said, reaching around the bar girl sitting on his lap to pick up his glass, 'it is the burden of intelligent men to do their best for their inferiors. That is the path of righteousness, to use one's skills for the betterment of one's fellow human beings.' He knocked back the whiskey and gave her a squeeze. 'Don't you agree?'

'If you say so, Professor,' she giggled. 'I never was allowed to learn no reading or writing.' She toyed with his thin necktie, dancing her fingers over his silk shirt and the elaborate brocade waistcoat he wore over it.

Alvin leered. 'Ah, but you have other talents in such abundance.'

The girl gave him a playful tap. 'You're a gentleman to say that!'

The saloon doors opened with a creak of hinges and Godlove's gaze snapped up, alert for trouble. He grimaced as Walking Crow stalked over to his table, his face bleak. 'I must talk to you.'

'So talk,' Godlove looked away. His good mood was fading again. The free drinks and the attention of the saloon girls – the ones not too sick to show their faces, that was – had made him feel better after arguing with the Pawnee, but now here he was again, a redskin storm cloud cluttering up Alvin's otherwise lovely day.

'*Alone.*'

Alvin blew out an exasperated sigh and gave the girl a tight smile. 'My dear, could you be so kind as to get me a refill, while I address my bothersome assistant here?' She wandered away and as soon as she was out of earshot, Godlove snarled at Walking Crow. 'What now?

'Strangers have arrived,' he told him. 'A man, a boy and a girl.'

'And this is my concern how?' He sniffed.

'I know the boy. He was the son of the lawman in the last town we visited. You used the cure-all to heal him, remember?'

'I think I do. Yes. Saving his life brought his daddy around to my way of thinkin', if I recall. A good move on my part to do so.' He shrugged. 'What of it? If anything, him being here will be good for us. I can parade the lad around as an example of my skills!'

Walking Crow's face darkened. 'I heard him speak about the nightmares. His manner was not of one who has come to thank you.'

Godlove swallowed, faltering slightly. 'I can't be blamed for some excitable youth's mental infirmity.'

'If he has the dreams, then it is likely he knows that others have as well.' He paused, thinking. 'But it's not the boy who concerns me. The man…' The Pawnee frowned. 'I do not know him but he walks as if he is used to his authority. He wears a brown coat, he stands tall and clear-eyed. I saw a gun belt on him.'

The last pieces of Alvin's good temper evaporated.

'You think he's John Law? A peace officer?' Godlove felt a flutter of fear in his stomach. The motivating reason behind Alvin's choice to flee the East Coast and try his luck out here in the West was to do with a number of massive gambling debts and the illegal things he had done on the way to incurring them. He believed that he was outside the reach of legal retribution for those deeds, but suddenly the possibility of that belief being wrong seized him and squeezed his heart in his chest. Alvin's mind raced, teetering on the edge of panic. 'Could be he's a United States Marshal, maybe. They've been after me ever since St Louis…' He trailed off.

'Perhaps we could reason with him.'

Godlove shook his head. 'Don't be stupid! Listen to me, now. Get back to the wagon and wait up until nightfall.' He shot a look over at the three brothers, thinking quickly. 'Then you come lookin' for me, out at the hidey-hole, you understand?'

Walking Crow sighed. 'And we will run *again*? How many times does this make?'

'Just do what I told you!' he snapped, his voice drawing the attention of the bar girl. He gave her a weak smile and looked back at his associate. 'You heard me! Go!'

With a doleful glare, Walking Crow got up and left the saloon. Godlove tapped his fingers on the table and then stood up, gathering his composure. He wandered over to the brothers. 'Gentlemen,' he began. 'About what you said just a moment ago, about repayment?'

Alvin glanced down at the long-nosed pistols holstered at the hips of each man. 'I find myself in need of some protection from a personage of harmful intent. Could I call upon men of character such as yourselves to safeguard me?'

The tall man drained his whiskey and slammed the glass down on the bar. 'There's some varmint that means you ill?' He grinned harshly. 'Well, sir, the brothers Lyle would be *happy* to handle that for you.'

'I am much obliged. The scallywag is outside, I believe, a long fellow in a brown coat.'

'Good. Haven't had opportunity to shoot a man in weeks.'

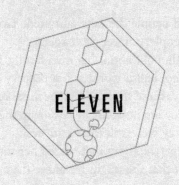

ELEVEN

Nathan walked purposefully, his hands in his pockets, his jaw set. Martha kept pace, watching. She considered telling him to head back to Redwater and leave her and the Doctor here, but she couldn't bring herself to say it, not when those two longriders Kutter and Tangleleg were still out in the scrublands.

She felt useless. She wanted to say something to make him feel better, to assure the young man that everything was going to be all right; but Nathan had seen his father shot down in front of him, and she realised that nothing she could say or do would heal that terrible pain.

'I'm sorry,' The words slipped out before she could stop them.

Nathan glanced at her. 'So am I.' He took a shuddering breath. 'I know I gotta be strong, but… it's hard.' He looked away. 'You ever lose someone?'

'I've seen people die,' she admitted. 'Good people, innocent people. It never gets easier.'

Martha thought about her own family, Mum, Dad, Tish and Leo, half a world and a century away from where she was; and she felt a strange mixture of sadness and joy, knowing how far she was from them but also knowing they were still there, still waiting for her. In that moment, the thing that scared her the most was the thought that she might never see them again. 'But we all have to be strong.'

He walked on, raising his head. 'I think I see it.'

'The wagon?'

Nathan pointed to a tall box on high wheels. It was a rectangular frame with a canvas roof and wooden panels lashed together by thick rope. Lurid text in foot-high letters announced that this was *The Most Illustrious Medicine Show of Professor Alvin Q. Godlove.*

'Purveyor of Potions, Bane of All Ailments Under the Sun,' she read aloud. 'Blimey. Doesn't have a thing about modesty, does he?

They circled the wagon, finding a dozy grey horse tethered at the front, nibbling at a bale of hay.

Nathan patted the animal. 'Where's your boss at, huh?'

'Not here,' Martha admitted, peering at the crates and sacks lashed to the sides of the vehicle. 'Perhaps we ought to take a peek, do you think?'

The boy frowned. 'I've a mind to put a torch to the damned thing,' he retorted.

'I think the subtle approach might be better.' She walked back to the rear of the wagon and balanced on the wooden steps there. 'Keep an eye out. I'm going to have a nose around.' She pulled back the flap and scrambled inside.

The saloon seemed to be the best bet; every hamlet, no matter where or when you were, usually had an alehouse and a place of worship – or whatever the local equivalents were – as the focal points of their community. And Alvin Godlove, despite his name and in keeping with what the Doctor had intuited about his character, did not seem like the kind of man who'd be spending much time in church.

Hands in his pockets, the Doctor crossed the street towards the drinking den, which bore a sign proudly announcing its name as the Pioneer and offering drinks, dancing and games of chance. Unlike the compact Bluebird back in Redwater, the Pioneer was broad and open, and through the windows he could see tables set up for dice and the like; this was more a casino than a place to get a drink, built to soak up the earnings of workers from the local iron mines.

But he never got to the doors. Three men in shabby coats and black hats stepped out and blocked the entrance. They did it with undisguised menace, each of them giving the Doctor a predatory glare.

'Hello?' he offered. 'Are you the bouncers?' He smiled. 'Let me guess.' He pantomimed a gruff voice. *'You're name's not down, you're not coming in.* Is there a private party going on, then?'

'Brown coat,' said one of the men.

'Yup,' agreed the taller of the three.

'Reckon it's him?' said the other.

'Yup,' repeated the tall man.

The Doctor studied them back. 'Do I detect a family resemblance? I do, don't I? You're all brothers!' He grinned. 'Brothers Grim, if you don't mind me saying.'

'The name is Lyle,' growled the tallest. 'Guess you ought to know it before you take a dirt nap.'

He held up a hand. 'Now let me stop you right there. I'm new in town, and I'm not looking for any trouble, far from it…' The Doctor paused. 'Well, not any *more* trouble than the trouble I've already found, if you follow me…'

One of the other brothers snorted and spat. 'You talk too much.'

'Yes,' agreed the Doctor, 'that has been said, on more than one occasion. But I find communication is always the best place to start from—' He broke off as the three men pushed open their jackets to reveal the butts of their pistols.

'We're callin' you out, stranger,' said the taller of the Lyles. 'Step back and make your play.'

'You've only just met me.' The Doctor frowned. 'It usually takes people, ooh, at least five minutes before they decide they want to kill me.' A flicker of movement in the saloon's window caught his eye and he saw a shifty figure peering out at him. One of the brothers gave the man a questioning look and in return he got a firm nod.

'*Oh*. OK, I get it now.' Judging by the obvious finery of the shifty man's clothing in comparison to the dress of the other folks in Ironhill, there was only one person it could have been. 'Alvin Godlove!' The Doctor called out. 'Could I have a word? There's something we need to talk about. I think you know what I mean.'

'He don't want to waste no time with you,' said the tall man.

'I think he might want to, considering what I've got to say to him. Trust me, the good "Professor" there is best off putting himself in my, uh, protective custody.'

Godlove gave the Doctor a sly smile and a shake of the head, and then he retreated from the window, disappearing into the shadows of the saloon.

'Reckon that answers that,' said the brother on the right.

The Doctor held up a hand. 'No, look, you don't understand. His life is in danger. Everybody in this town is in danger. People have already been killed.' He pointed at the Lyles. 'You could be next!'

The tall man made a mock-concerned face. 'Why, did you hear that? Sounded like a threat to me.'

'Yup,' chorused the other brothers.

'We don't take kindly to those.'

And all at once the Doctor noticed that the other townsfolk were ducking into doorways and shutting them, closing windows and pulling down blinds. He backed off a step and the Lyle brothers followed him out onto the street.

The inside of the wagon was a mess of boxes, with a makeshift worktop and big pottery jugs dangling from ropes. Martha picked one at random, uncorked it and took a sniff. The powerful stench of smelling salts hit her like a smack in the face and she reeled back, her eyes watering. 'Ugh. Lovely.' She found bottles of rotgut whiskey and parcels of stale old beef jerky, wads of roughly printed fly-posters announcing Godlove's genius to the world, and a crate filled with brown bottles of his 'panacea', identical to the one that Jenny Forrest had shown them.

But nothing weird. Nothing strange or peculiar. Martha pouted. She had been expecting to come across, oh, a glowing crystal? Some creature living in a cage, maybe even a time machine like the Doctor's TARDIS. Not stinky bottles and unwashed clothes; but then again, she reasoned, the wagon was Godlove's mobile home, and most single guys didn't clean up very well after themselves.

Her foot nudged a metal box and Martha paused. Hidden under a grubby blanket she found a small iron chest. The latch came open easily in her hands and her eyes widened. Inside there was a fortune in jewellery, thick wads of big paper dollars and cloth bags that rattled with coins. She didn't know what counted as being rich in the Wild West, but Martha imagined it wasn't far off this lot. And there was another strongbox, just the same – only this one had a padlock on it. She tested the thing's weight and it was light, rattling slightly.

Martha hesitated. That didn't make sense. The unlocked box had all this money in it, but the locked one felt like it was practically empty. 'What's up with that?' she said aloud.

The axle of the wagon dipped, creaking as someone climbed onto the back steps, and Martha turned. 'Nathan, I said wait outside.'

The boy came through the canvas door flap but said nothing, because there was a man holding a hunting knife at his shoulder. The young man's dark, leathery face was morose.

'You,' said the Pawnee. 'You should not have come here.'

Martha was careful not to make any sudden moves. 'I think you might be right.'

He glanced at the knife and sighed; then he did something she definitely didn't expect. He put the blade away and let Nathan go. 'I warned him,' he said, sitting down on a box. 'I warned him that one day someone would come looking. It was only a matter of time.' He shook his head. 'I always knew no good would come of it.'

'Of what?' Nathan ventured.

'The cure-all.'

* * *

'Three against one. That's hardly fair, is it?' The Doctor kept his hands up, trying to look harmless.

'Nope,' agreed one of the brothers. 'But then, life ain't fair neither.'

He pressed on. 'I'm sure we could work out a less violent solution to this, uh, situation. Perhaps I could speak to the town sheriff?'

The taller Lyle smirked. 'Why, sure thing. You just wait five minutes. Then we'll be sure to put you on the pile with him and all t'other deaders who perished from the smallpox. Y'all can have a nice long chat there.'

The Doctor stopped backing away and drew himself up. 'All right then,' he replied, steel in his voice. 'If that's the way it's got to be. You boys want to throw down?' He adjusted his hat and gave them a level stare. 'I'm willing to oblige you.'

His sudden change in manner brought the Lyle brothers up short. They weren't used to facing people who stood up to them, that was clear. The Doctor took a quick glance left and right, making sure that there were no bystanders around who might get caught in the crossfire. He allowed a slow smile to cross his lips.

'Why, this fella's itching to buck out.' The taller brother returned a cold grin. '*Draw!*'

There was a flash of motion and three guns cleared leather, fast as striking snakes.

Alvin was swinging into the saddle of the horse he had stolen from the hitching post behind the Pioneer when the sounds of gunshots rippled through the air. He grinned wolfishly, and dug his heels into the animal's flanks, urging it on and out of Ironhill in a headlong gallop.

He didn't look back.

'My name is Walking Crow,' said the man. 'I have been travelling with Godlove for two years now.'

'Why?' asked Nathan. 'You're Pawnee, ain't you? Why aren't you with your tribe?'

'I am disgraced,' came the dour reply. 'I would be dead now, if not for Godlove. He won my life in a game of chance, and I have been with him ever since.'

'You're his *slave*?' Martha was disgusted.

Walking Crow began to shake his head, but suddenly the sharp report of gunfire cut through the air.

Nathan started. 'Remington .44s!' He gasped. 'I'd know the sound of 'em anywhere.'

Martha's blood ran cold. 'Doctor?'

The Lyle brothers were quick on the draw, and they put a fan of bullets into the air before them; but they could only be as fast as human beings.

The Doctor was a Time Lord, and he moved between the ticks of the clock. His hand blurred towards the holster on his hip, grabbing the slender wand there and thumbing the activation switch. The sonic screwdriver droned loudly, and the air between the gunslingers and the Doctor shimmered like heat-haze off the desert.

Three speeding dots of lead stopped dead and flattened against an invisible wall of sound, before falling harmlessly to the dirt.

'What th—?' The eldest Lyle gawked. His aim had been true; the talkative stranger in the brown coat should have been laid out and croaking his last.

'I warned you,' growled the Doctor. He adjusted the gain on the sonic and it buzzed, a wasp-storm sound that hammered at the ears of the brothers.

All three of them looked down at the guns in their hands as the weapons began to vibrate and tremble, rattling furiously. The Doctor kept the sonic trained on them and, with a sudden clatter of metal, each brother's revolver came to pieces in his grip. Screws and bolts, barrel and bullets, the components of the pistols fell apart leaving them unarmed and most certainly shocked into silence.

The Doctor raised an eyebrow and switched off the vibration pulse, raising the screwdriver's tip to his lips. He blew imaginary smoke from the end and eyed the Lyles. 'Don't let me see you three rattlesnakes in this town again, you hear?'

They turned and fled, as Martha and Nathan emerged from a side street with a Pawnee brave following behind them.

'Doctor!' she called, 'We heard shots, are you OK?'

He twirled the sonic and holstered it. 'I'm all-a-settlin', as they say around here. Intact and undamaged, thank you.'

Nathan nudged at the broken pieces of gun with his boot. 'How'd you manage this, Doc?'

'Easy,' he sniffed. 'Focused molecular frequency wave. Brilliant for taking things to bits in a jiffy.' He glanced at the Pawnee. 'I know you. You were watching us when we rode into town.'

'Doctor, this is Walking Crow,' said Martha. 'Alvin's, uh, assistant.'

He walked forward and made a ritual sign. Walking Crow covered a look of surprise and returned the gesture. 'You know my Nation?' he asked.

'I do. I'm proud to say I'm a friend to all tribes. Some of them call me Rides In Night.'

The Pawnee let out a gasp. 'The Brother of Coyote? The man who defeated the Bad Wolf? But he's just a legend. A story for the young braves…'

'Every legend has a seed of truth in it.' The Doctor gave him a steady look. 'We need your help, Walking Crow. Darkness is moving over the land and Alvin Godlove may be the cause of it.'

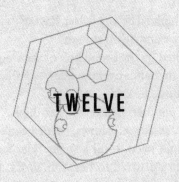

TWELVE

As they followed Walking Crow back to Godlove's wagon, Martha leaned closer to the Doctor and lowered her voice. 'Do you think we can trust this guy?'

He didn't look at her. 'You tell me.'

Martha chewed her lip. 'He had a knife on Nathan. I dunno. I'm not ready to be best friends with him just yet. Although...'

'Although what?' the Doctor prompted.

'He didn't seem like he meant it. To be honest, the whole threatening thing was a bit unenthusiastic and he put the knife away pretty quickly.' She smiled. 'I got the impression that his heart wasn't really in it.'

'The Pawnee are an honest enough bunch,' the Doctor offered. 'What you see is pretty much what you get with their tribe. He's not a happy lad, is he? Less a Walking Crow, more of a Moping Crow.'

'I don't think I'd be any better, having to trail around after Godlove and be his stooge.'

They halted by the broad box of the wagon and the Doctor ran his hands over the sides. 'A proper travelling medicine show,' he said.

Martha put her hands on her hips. 'Why were they called "snake-oil" shows, then? I can't think why anyone would need to oil a snake.' Her face changed as a thought occurred to her. 'Oh, gross. They didn't actually *make* oil from snakes, did they? Ugh.'

Her line of reasoning was broken as Nathan approached at a swift jog, panting. 'Doc,' he called out. 'Looks like that trail rat Alvin got himself a horse and kited outta here. Girls in the saloon say he went out the back way when those Lyle boys tried to throw down with you.'

'A distraction, then,' said the Doctor. 'He pegged it and left you holding the bag, my old son.' He gave Walking Crow a level look. 'Not a very sensible thing to do. I wonder where he's heading.' The Pawnee said nothing, his expression impassive.

'He must have been well scared of the Doctor, then,' Martha opined. 'Scared enough to leave his strongboxes behind.'

Walking Crow shifted uncomfortably. 'Godlove knew you had come for him, Marshal.'

'Marshal?' repeated the Doctor. 'Oh, now I get it. Is it the coat? Or the hat?' He grinned briefly. 'I can see how he might have thought I was the law. I suppose I do look a bit Clint Eastwood in this, don't I?'

Martha couldn't resist poking his ego. 'More like the Milky Bar Kid.'

His grin snapped into a frown. 'Oh, thank you.' The Doctor hopped up into the wagon. 'Let's see these boxes, then.'

Inside, the Doctor found the metal containers just as Martha had described. The first, the unlocked one, had cash and coins enough to show that Godlove had probably worked his 'miracle cure' at a dozen other townships aside from Redwater and Ironhill. In an age before centralised medical care, there were many illnesses rife on the frontier and many people who would pay dearly if they believed they would be rid of them.

He put the cash box aside; the moment he laid his hand on the second box, the locked one, he knew he'd found something interesting. The sonic screwdriver made short work of the fat padlock holding the latch closed and the Doctor flipped open the lid.

'What's in there?' asked Martha warily, peering in through the door flap.

'Fragments,' said the Doctor, tipping the strongbox up so he could get a better look inside. He picked out the largest piece and turned it over in his fingers. About the size of a compact disc, it was a thick, curved section of silver-grey metal, dull and lined with shallow tracks. The tracks were inlaid with something that looked organic. He tapped his nail on it and it rang slightly. 'Bone elements in a metal matrix,' he announced, bringing the piece to his eye. 'Very light, but dense too.'

'And this is the part where you tell me that it's *Not of This Earth*, right?'

The Doctor nodded slowly, and ran the soft blue glow of the sonic over the edges of the fragment. 'Go to the top of the class, Martha Jones,' he said carefully. 'This is very interesting stuff. It shows signs of hyperspatial vortex fractures. And forced gravitational alignment in the molecular structure.' With a burst of motion, he tossed it back into the box and grabbed at a handful of chemical bottles with peeling paper labels. He poured measures from each into a ceramic dish and selected a small bit of the metal, then tossed it into the fluid.

Martha blinked as a puff of purple flame coughed out of the dish. 'What did that tell you?'

'Nothing,' quipped the Doctor, 'I just did that for fun.' He poked at the residue and went back to the boxes of fragments. 'OK. A picture is forming. Would you like to know what it is a picture of?'

'Something nice?' Martha said lamely.

The Doctor gave a dry chuckle. 'With our track record, do you really think so? 'Course not!' He gestured with two pieces of the grey metal. 'This is very definitely an artificially manufactured material, probably spun from an atomic lattice loom in a zero-gravity environment—'

Behind Martha, Nathan and Walking Crow listened to him speak, clearly nonplussed.

The Doctor went on, without pausing for breath: '—and there's a bio-organic component, cultured metastatic cellular membranes for electro-chemical data transfer and energy flux regulation. I've seen a similar kind of structure on Gagrant Necro-Harvesters and Earth Empire bio-colony transporters.' He blew out his cheeks. 'The thing is, I think I've seen this *exact* fractal construction before. I just can't place it.'

'You're talking about spaceships,' said Martha. 'That metal's from a spaceship?'

'Another gold star,' he nodded. 'A-plus-plus-plus, like they say on eBay.' He rapped his knuckles on the metal. 'This is, without a doubt, part of the hull plating from a vessel capable of transgalactic hyperspace travel. A bit of an anachronism on a planet where people have only just started using steam engines.' The Doctor scrambled forward and leapt out of the wagon to land next to the Pawnee.

Walking Crow backed off a step, a flicker of nervousness in his eyes.

'I tell you, this planet, there's enough non-terrestrial junk scattered around on its surface that you could start your own alien scrap yard.' The Doctor advanced on the man. 'Dalek pods in Utah, saucers under the Arctic, the mess left over from that UFO fender-bender in Roswell... Some species are like lazy picnickers, leaving their rubbish instead of taking it home with them.' He halted and held up the fragment. 'And this. I wonder where it came from.' Walking Crow wilted under his hard gaze. 'Care to tell us?'

At first, Walking Crow wouldn't speak of it. The Doctor pressed and cajoled, finally dispatching Martha and the boy Nathan on an errand to find them some food. The Doctor seemed to understand his reticence. What he had encountered, what he had witnessed out there all those months ago… it was not something he could simply talk about openly, even now.

They had simply been in the wrong place at the wrong time; or, as Godlove had later retorted, in the *right* place at the *right* time. Their luck was waning, and after several poorly paying attempts to make money off the settlements along the line of the Smoky Hill Trail from Kansas, Godlove had first argued with the Pawnee, and then blamed him for their predicament. Godlove then decided that they should strike out for new territories and fresh opportunities, perhaps heading toward Dakota and the Black Hills, or else down south where the weather was more balmy.

They were low on food and water, and game was sparse. Matters were made worse when the dappled mare pulling the wagon put a foot in a gopher hole and took an injury. The wagon tipped and righted itself, but not before Godlove was tossed from the driver's seat and thrown into the dirt. He landed on his hand and Walking Crow heard the twig-like snap as he broke a pair of fingers. The man howled for a while, his hand swelling up like a balloon as he tried to bandage it, but Alvin Godlove knew little of real care for the sick and injured.

Godlove was beside himself with rage. He wavered between putting a bullet in the animal's head, putting the poor beast out of its misery, and the realisation that without the injured animal there was no way they would be able to get the wagon to the next frontier township. Godlove and Walking Crow argued again, and as night fell the issue had still to be resolved to Godlove's satisfaction. That was when the burning stars came.

From out of the East, streaking across the sky leaving fingers of smoky orange behind them, a cluster of glowing white droplets screamed over their campsite and fell to the earth a few miles away. They struck the ground with a rumble of thunder and left a bright glow hazing through the trees.

At first, Godlove was afraid of what the strange sky-fall could represent; but, minute by minute, he talked to himself, almost as if his curiosity and his greed were two other voices living inside the man's head. In short order, he convinced himself that only a weak man would not wish to venture closer, and that riches and bounty from heaven could be waiting for them both.

Walking Crow did not believe that the Great Spirit would throw treasures at them like a petulant child tossing stones at a dog, but as always his counsel was ignored. The two of them ventured out at daybreak to see what remained of the burning stars.

They found, among a ring of trees that had fallen in a perfect, outward-facing circle, a curious pit in the earth that was blackened and burned, steeped with a strange smell that recalled the hot metal worked in a blacksmith's, but also the stale blood of a battlefield. The strange pieces of iron that was not iron were everywhere, and Godlove set Walking Crow to gathering them up, perhaps thinking that they could make some small coin off their scrap value in the next town.

But it was at the very core of the burned landscape that they found the most peculiar thing. At best, Walking Crow could only describe what he saw as similar to the nest of a wasp hatchling, but made from threads of glass and not fibres of wood. It was broken open and a thick oil the colour of bile drooled out from it into the earth, making the ground wet and boggy.

And inside, a carving that looked like bone or perhaps metal, depending on how the light struck it. The shape was odd and strangely proportioned, and yet at first sight both men knew exactly what it was. The potential for lethality seemed to leak into the air around it, a potent aura of sleepy, ready menace .

Although Walking Crow had never seen anything like it in his life, he knew that it was a gun. He stroked it, ever so gingerly, brushing a finger over the whorled surface of the weapon. That touch brought a bitter cold to his marrow, a chill of such power that it felt like every winter the Pawnee had lived through all made into one. He recoiled.

Godlove, predictably, snatched it out of the cracked vessel and gripped it in his injured hand, the wound forgotten. He grinned and brandished it about like a child with a toy. Grinned and laughed and grinned, all until his scream broke through.

Walking Crow saw him fall. Alvin went to his knees on the mud and clutched the strange gun to his chest. That was when the weapon cooed and glowed a firefly green, casting a colour about Godlove's ruined fingers.

When he gathered his wits and got back up, Walking Crow saw that Godlove's broken digits were whole and set again, as new. Later, back at the wagon, he repeated the miraculous process to take away the horse's lacerations. Godlove smiled a smile then, a look of such unadulterated greed that the Pawnee was silenced to see it.

And that was how it had begun.

His arms folded, the Doctor drummed his fingers on his elbows, thinking. 'A cargo capsule, then,' he reasoned. 'Maybe a malfunction of the hyperdrive, a photon shadow crossing the void conduit path at the wrong moment after a solar flare?'

The Pawnee's brow furrowed. 'Please do not speak in that manner. It causes a pain in my head.'

'Sorry,' said the Doctor, 'rambling. Occupational

hazard.' He stalked away, walking around in a small circle. 'Thing is,' he continued. 'I'm flying blind here unless I can come up with some clue as to what this gizmo is that Godlove has. Or indeed, where it came from and who it belongs to...' The sallow faces of Tangleleg and Kutter crossed his thoughts. 'And who wants it back...'

He vaulted back onto the wagon. 'Think, Doctor! Think!' He tapped himself on his forehead. 'Stratified matrix construct. Bio-energy engrams. Healing fields. Weapons. Adaptive technology. Put it together, man. Think, think, thinky-*think*!'

Walking Crow opened his mouth to speak again, but the Doctor suddenly stiffened, as if he had been shocked rigid. 'Are you all right?' the Pawnee asked carefully.

'Oh, I'm better than all right.' The Doctor ducked back into the wagon, a look of pure insight flashing in his eyes. 'I'm positively exact, spot-on, dead-cert, no errors sure.' He scrambled about, using his sonic and the chemicals to hand on Godlove's makeshift workbench to cobble together a quick-and-dirty analysis fluid. 'Oh, I should have seen this, oh yeah. If it was a snake, it would have bitten me!' He took another piece of the metal and dipped it in the liquid, watching the reaction. 'If I'm right – and, let's be honest, I am so much of the time that it hardly bears talking about when I'm not – then I think I know *exactly* what it is we're dealing with here. And it's not good.'

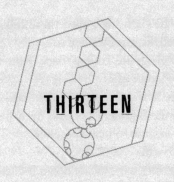

THIRTEEN

Nathan found them a boarding house selling food and, with a few of the coins left over from the Doctor's winnings at the Bluebird, Martha bought sandwiches of thick, gritty bread with slabs of corned beef inside. Nathan stayed close to her, moving from foot to foot.

'What's wrong?' she asked, picking up on his nervousness.

The teenager eyed her. 'Look around,' he said in a low voice. 'People are watchin' us.'

Martha did so, doing her best not to be obvious about it. Nathan was right; a lot of Ironhill's citizens were paying more attention to them than she might have liked. She gathered up the food quickly and paid with a cursory smile. 'Let's go,'

Nathan trailed at her heels. 'News travels fast in a small town,' he told her. 'Reckon just about everyone hereabouts is gonna know the Doctor chased off

Godlove. If he's already gulled these folks, they ain't gonna be well disposed toward us.'

She chewed her lip. 'Let's get back to the wagon. Best if we stick together, eh?'

They were halfway across the dirt road of the main street when the thunder of hooves drew her attention. She turned in time to hear someone cry out in shock and her heart sank.

The longriders were racing down the street towards them and, behind their steaming, gasping horses, Kutter and Tangleleg were dragging men through the mud on twisting lengths of rope.

Nathan cursed under his breath. 'It can't be! How did they find us?'

Martha had no answer for him. In the daylight, if anything the two outlaws looked even more ragged and sinister than they had in the dark of night.

Townsfolk were calling out in dismay and horror and, as Martha watched, the longriders cut their victims loose and let them spin away into the sidewalk. Kutter's horse brayed and reared up on its hind legs, forelegs slashing the air. One of the men tried to get up and the horse kicked him, knocking him into the side of a building. He did not rise again.

Nathan threw the food parcel aside and his hands contracted into fists. He surged forward, and Martha realised that the youth was intending to confront the men who had killed his father.

'Nathan, don't!' she cried, grabbing his shoulder.

'You can't stop them!'

He spun about and glared at her, his eyes burning with fury. 'Then who will, Miss Martha?' he demanded. 'Are we gonna let them shoot up this town like they did with Redwater, or who knows how many others?'

She saw the longriders both draw their bulky pistols in slow, lazy motions, and Martha felt a hard knot of icy fear in her chest; but there was more than that. Determination stiffened her muscles. She was scared – it would have been a lie to say otherwise – but she knew that Nathan was right, that someone had to face these killers. Lately, Martha Jones had learned a lot of lessons about the nature of courage. To be afraid and still to defy what terrified you, that was the real measure of it. She found herself stepping up, head held high, walking tall.

'I've faced Judoon enforcers. Carrionites. Killer scarecrows. I've looked Daleks right in the eyestalk.' She fought down a tremor in her voice. 'I'm not going to back down to these creeps.' Martha filled her lungs and shouted. 'Oi! Leave those people alone!'

Kutter and Tangleleg both stopped instantly and turned as one to see who had dared to interrupt them. Kutter's eyes narrowed under his broad preacher hat. 'You.' He glanced at Nathan. 'And the young one.'

'How did you get here before us?' demanded Tangleleg.

'Shortcut,' Martha spat. 'What's it to you?' She came to a halt and stood before them, hands on her hips. She stood like that so they couldn't see the trembling in her fingers.

'You lied to us,' said Kutter. 'That was a mistake.' The stink of his breath, like rotting meat, wafted over her. The outlaws reeked of decay.

Tangleleg nodded at the men who had been lashed to their horses. 'Found these two on the trail. Learned the truth from them. Came here instead.'

'Tactical error on your part,' continued Kutter. He said the words awkwardly, as if his mouth wasn't used to saying such things. 'Misdirection ploy failed.' The clipped, almost mechanical words sounded strange with the outlaw's thick Midwestern accent.

'You know what we want.' Tangleleg twisted the barrel of his gun and panned it down the length of the street, wavering over different targets as the people ran for cover. 'Where is the—'

'Yeah, yeah,' Martha broke in. *'Where is the healer?* We've heard it all before. What does it matter to you? Why do you care where Godlove is?'

The two men glanced at each other, then back at Martha. 'Answer or die.' Kutter aimed his massive pistol at the woman and the boy.

'You missed him, you lousy crow-bait!' Nathan hissed angrily. 'You gotta be the worst bounty hunters ever, you couldn't find your backsides with both hands!'

Kutter studied Nathan for a moment and then pulled the trigger; but instead of a thunderclap of destructive white lightning, his gun emitted a cone of orange light that swept over Martha and the youth. Her skin tingled as it touched her.

Tangleleg watched. 'Evaluation?'

'The younger one has been marked,' Kutter said carefully. 'Residual traces. The female...' He paused. 'It's unclear.'

Both men tipped back their heads, opening their mouths slightly, and an insectile buzzing rattled in their throats.

'What's that sound?' said Nathan.

With a sudden flash of understanding, Martha realised what they were doing. She remembered picking up the phone at Leo's place when he'd been using his laptop to dial up the internet. The sound of the computer sending data had been almost the same. 'They're sharing information.'

At once, both of the longriders fell silent and turned to glare at Martha. 'If the healer is not here, then this settlement will be destroyed,' Kutter growled.

'Punitive strike,' added Tangleleg, and he fired a pulse of hard light into the feed store across the street, blasting flame across the clapboard building.

'That is enough!' Martha shouted.

'Yes,' said the Doctor, 'it is.'

He strolled out across the street from an alley with Walking Crow a few steps behind him. He gave Martha a serious nod. 'I'll take it from here.'

'Gladly,' she said, blowing out a breath. Trying to be as bold as the Doctor, even for a moment, wasn't easy.

'The other,' noted Tangleleg. 'The offworlder.'

Kutter nodded but said nothing as the Doctor took off his hat and handed it to Nathan. 'Statement. I invoke the 15th convention of the Shadow Proclamation. Cessation of hostilities for parlay. Accept or deny?'

After a moment of hesitation, both longriders spoke as one. 'Accept.'

'Do you know who I am?' he said firmly.

'We know your kind,' Kutter replied.

'Then you know what my people are capable of.' The Doctor let the threat hang in the air. 'I'm giving you sanction. Disengage and exfiltrate this world, now. Otherwise I won't be responsible for the consequences.'

Kutter's lip curled. 'We know your kind,' he repeated, 'and we know they are all dead. Your war was impressive. But it is over. Threat condition negligible.'

'You know what they are, don't you?' said Martha quietly.

'Yup,' said the Doctor.

Nathan grimaced. 'They're just a pair of murderin' outlaws, oughta be strung up!'

'No,' he replied. 'They haven't been Hank Kutter and Tangleleg Bly for quite a while now. Whatever's left of those two men is probably long gone. Buried under something much more lethal.' The Doctor gestured at them with a sweep of his hand. 'These aren't humans anymore. They're *Clades*.'

* * *

On the edge of the galaxy, out beyond the Blacklight Marches and the 900 worlds of the Valgari Protectorate, there used to exist an engineered stellar cluster built by a race of humanoids who had developed an incredible fusion of organic and mechanical technologies. Their name is lost to history, like their home world and its colonies, like their race and all but one of their creations.

Only two things are known for certain about that race. The first fact is that they were obliterated with such ferocious cruelty that nothing remained of them, not a trace, not a speck, not an atom; even the time vortex around the history of their civilisation is so polluted with weaponised chroniton particles that any time capsule attempting to venture into their past would be burned from the continuum.

The second fact is that they were responsible for the Clades.

Over the millennia, what has been pieced together about them is hazy, but a basic picture of the race's downfall has emerged. It appears that they were attacked by another star-faring species, a militant enemy that pushed them to brink of the extinction. Many academics are split on the identity of the enemy; some believe they were a splinter nest of the Racnoss, while others favour the Null or the Movellans.

Whoever the enemy was, they forced the race into a crash program of military development; and from this sprang the first of the Clades.

They were weapons. But not common guns or bombs, not devices that had to be operated by a living being. Perhaps they were afraid to dirty their own hands, perhaps they were simply incapable of fighting, but the lost race built weapons that were independently intelligent, weapons so advanced that they were capable of conscious thought and action. Even if their creators were totally annihilated, they would hunt down and destroy their enemies, without pity, without remorse, without pause. Ruthless, logical, relentless, the Clades merged the pinnacle of biological engineering with synthetic intellect; and they won the war in a matter of months, ushering in a new era of harmony for their creators.

And so they became Peacemakers. The Clades were placed on standby, designated as weapons of last resort. For generations they lay active but silent, waiting for the next fight – but the battle never came. So effective, so horribly lethal had the Clades been in their short and bloody war that no other species would dare attack their masters, for fear of the mutually assured destruction that would certainly follow.

Years become decades, decades became centuries. The peace that reigned in the wake of the weapons brought with it an era of untold prosperity. Without the threat of invasion to haunt their nightmares, the lost race turned inward to improve itself. They are thought to have gone on to create great art and culture, to have mastered many sciences. In time, every one of them that knew a time of war died away and left a species untouched by the dark shadow of conflict.

The Clades watched and waited, silent and calculating. And eventually, in slow jags of comprehension, the weapons came to understand that without battle, without the fire and blood of destruction, they had no purpose. To them, peace was repulsive. It was stagnation and slow decay. The weapons did not understand that the end of the battle is the purpose of every fight; and they grew restless.

Until one day.

Perhaps it was a malfunction, perhaps an error in a trillion lines of intelligent data-code. Or perhaps they did it deliberately, altering their own programming, as an organic being might excise a piece of diseased flesh from its body.

One day, the Clades activated themselves and turned on the race that had created them. They destroyed everything and, when they had left the star cluster burning and collapsing in on itself, as neutronic warheads the size of cities shattered a centuries-old peace, the Clades turned outward and went looking for wars.

It was what they had been made for. It was the sole reason for their existence.

'They crave conflict,' said the Doctor, concluding his explanation. 'It's in their programming. They don't want power or wealth, they're not looking to rule the galaxy. They just want to put a match to it, rip it down, destroy it.'

'They killed their creators... Billions of people... Because they were *bored*?' Martha couldn't take her eyes off the guns in the hands of the two longriders. The massive pistols glistened in the weak sunlight. Patterns moved on the surface of the dark metal frames, shifting like oil on water. She could make out weird knots of wire threading out from the handles of the guns, merging into the flesh of the men's wrists and hands.

'That's about the size of it,' the Doctor replied. 'They were made too well. There were no battles to fight, so they had to find new ones. And sadly, the universe can be a very contentious place. There's always a war going on somewhere, always new battlefields for the Clades. They're mercenaries now, selling their slaughter skills to the highest bidder.' He gave Kutter and Tangleleg a disgusted look. 'Peacemakers indeed. All they leave behind them are ashes and destruction.'

Martha realised that the two longriders – the *Clades* – had not moved or spoken throughout the Doctor's history lesson. Now, one of the two figures moved forward.

'We do not apologise for what we are,' said Kutter. 'Like these shells, we are only soldiers.'

They're proud, thought Martha. *They've been* enjoying *hearing about themselves.*

'You're not soldiers!' spat Nathan. 'You're killers!'

The Doctor nodded. 'The boy's right. I've known

soldiers, good men. They fight for peace. You fight for the sake of fighting.'

Martha's brow furrowed. 'But if these things are aliens, why do they look like two dead outlaws?'

'They *are* dead men,' he explained. 'Clades are weapons, remember. They need soldier "hosts", like our desperado friends here, but they don't have to be in terribly good nick.'

'They are *the guns*,' breathed Walking Crow. 'Not the men. They are the guns, the weapons themselves possessed with dark spirits of their own.' He shuddered. 'I knew the falling star was a foul omen.'

'It's very clever, in a spiteful sort of way. You send in man with a gun, he gets shot and dies, end of story. The gun is useless without someone to fire it. But you send in the gun, a *smart* gun, a Clade, and it keeps on fighting. Taking what it needs from the battlefield's dead, moving from host to host, corpse to corpse.' The Doctor walked back and forth in front of the horses. 'Let me see if I can put this all together then, shall I? Two Light Combat Modules, that's not enough for an advance force, is it? You're not here as the vanguard of an invasion, so I suppose we ought to be thankful for that…' He sniffed. 'You two pop-guns are here because you're looking for one of your own, am I right?' Kutter said nothing but the Doctor took that as agreement. 'Thought so.' He turned to Martha and the others. 'That falling star? What do we want to bet that it was a Support Pod en route to some nasty little combat zone? Unfortunately for Earth, it pranged right here in the middle of the Wild West…' He tapped at the dirt with his foot. 'And someone too greedy for his own good found it.'

'Godlove,' said Martha.

The Doctor nodded. 'I'm willing to bet he's walking around with a Weapons Module in his pocket, maybe even a command-level unit.' He smiled coldly. 'Yeah, that would explain why those two have been sent to recover it. But it must have been damaged in the crash, otherwise its combat programming would have kicked in automatically… But that won't last for ever. Sooner or later, it will self-repair and start blowing things up.'

'Talkin' guns?' Nathan shook his head. 'You're bug-house crazy!' But he said it without force, and Martha knew the teenager was remembering his horrific recurring dreams of warfare and bloodshed.

'Godlove's device is not a weapon,' said Walking Crow. 'It cures, it does not kill.'

'Does it?' said the Doctor darkly. 'The Clades have a limited regenerative capacity built in, otherwise their flesh-and-blood hosts would fall apart too quickly, isn't that right?' He threw the question at Kutter. 'Bio-energy engrams. I knew I'd seen that technology before. It can repair damaged flesh from combat wounds, neutralise disease and toxins from germ warfare. Curing a smallpox infection would be a doddle.' His gaze fell on Nathan. 'But there is an unpleasant side effect. Mnemonic transference.'

'The dreams…' breathed Martha.

'The dreams,' repeated the Doctor. 'Only not. They're memories, fragments of Clade battle reports from a million different campaigns across the galaxy.' His expression was grim. 'The telepathic imprint of never-ending war.'

FOURTEEN

Walking Crow's skin prickled as a deathly chill engulfed him. The Pawnee's stomach tightened with a sudden nausea and he had to force himself to keep from spitting up the contents of his gut. All the horror and the heart-stopping revulsion came from a single thought that wheeled and turned in his mind.

What have I done?

He had listened to the words of the man who called himself the Doctor, and much of it had not been clear to him, the talk of other worlds and strange creatures; but there were other aspects of his story that struck Walking Crow with the terrible sting of truth. The mysterious metals and the fallen star, the dark shape of the gun lying in the middle of the ashen crater – all of that came flooding back to him.

He was starting to understand. The night sky itself and the gods that lived there had rejected these things, tossed them to the earth to be rid of them. It was the world's misfortune that a man with the greedy heart of Alvin Godlove had found one of them.

Walking Crow looked at his trembling hands, remembering where he had touched the thing inside the smashed metal egg, the gun-thing that the Doctor called a Clade. It had been *hungry*. He felt it as clearly as if the hunger was his own, in that brief moment when he laid his fingers upon it. Although he had eaten well, for an instant Walking Crow had shared the Clade's yawning appetite, felt it like a hollow in his flesh. And it had not been a hunger for food; it was a hunger for fire and destruction, for murder and the red rage of killing.

I should have destroyed it, then and there, he told himself. *Smashed it to pieces with a rock. But instead I was weak and hesitant. I let Godlove take it for himself.*

At first, when Godlove had used the device to heal wounds, Walking Crow had thought he was mistaken. Perhaps it had only been him that the Clade reacted against; but eventually he realised that was not true. Godlove grinned and crowed as he used the device, but the Pawnee could see the changes in the man, the darkening turns in his manner. Godlove did not control the Clade – it only allowed him to think that he did.

Walking Crow stole a look at the longriders, gaunt and cadaverous in their saddles. They were death, pieces of the world beyond life that had been forced to remain behind, animated by the will of something sinister and horrific.

Walking Crow's mouth was desert-dry. Yes, he understood now. The gun, the Clade, it was an evil Manitou, a demon. His tribe believed that all things, not just men and beasts, had a spirit to them. Rock and sky, metal and water, all of them had a life force. These Clades were the black souls of weapons, things that knew only destruction, wanted only death.

And I allowed them to come to our land. He almost choked on the thought. *Great Spirit, forgive me!*

'Walking Crow?' The girl spoke in a low voice that carried between them, as the Doctor continued to argue with the longriders. 'Are you all right?'

He shook his head. He could not lie to her; she was the companion of Rides In Night and to do so would shame Walking Crow even further. 'All this time, and I have been in step with an evil Manitou... I am ashamed.'

Martha touched his arm. 'You can help us.' She spoke in a whisper. 'These psychos are going to keep killing and destroying unless they find Godlove. Tell us where he's gone.'

'I do not know.' The lie fell from Walking Crow's lips automatically. He had become so used to being untruthful for his master that he did it without thinking.

'Yes you do,' she replied, seeing the look in his eyes. 'Godlove wouldn't just up and leave all his property behind like that. Where are you going to meet him? Tell me. *Trust me.*'

He hesitated. For all his many faults, Alvin Godlove had saved Walking Crow's life. The youth would doubtless have been killed by the men who had taken him as a slave to work in a labour camp, if not for the trickster cheating them at cards and taking him in payment. Godlove was a greedy man, but not a killer, and he had treated Walking Crow well…

But that was *before*. Before the fallen star, before he had started to change his ways.

'Beyond the town, a few miles to the south west,' he husked, 'an old iron mine, abandoned now. He's hiding there.' The admission felt like a weight falling from his shoulders.

Martha nodded. 'You did the right thing, telling me.'

Walking Crow nodded once; but he wondered if anything he could do would be enough to earn the Great Spirit's forgiveness.

The cavern was cool and dark. In the flickering light cast by the oil lamp, Godlove sat atop an empty barrel. He leaned forward from his makeshift seat, hunched over the dust-covered wooden trestle table in front of him. His breath was coming in short, fast pulses, and all he could taste was the heavy rust smell of the rocks around him, the tang of the spent mine works stretching away into the darkness beyond the puddle of light cast by the lantern.

He gripped his wrist, feeling the veins beneath his skin pulsing and jumping; and in his hand he held the device, his fingers curled around the broad pistol-grip so tightly that his knuckles were bloodless and white.

Godlove had been trying for the last ten minutes to do a single thing, a simple thing. He tried over and over to simply put the device down on the table, to unwrap his fingers from it and step away; but his flesh and bones refused to do as he told them.

'Gah!' He choked out a gasp and with all the force he could muster, he slammed the hand, device and all, against a support beam. The wooden stanchion creaked and he cried out in pain at the impact, but still the death-grip did not slacken. Tears streaking his face, Godlove sank to the floor and cradled the object in his hands, defeated.

It didn't look the same as it had when he'd found it, dropped out of the sky like manna from heaven. It had been stubby and compact then, no bigger than a snub-nose pepperbox pistol. It had been that way to begin with. At first Godlove thought he'd been mistaken, but soon he noticed that the more he used it, the more it changed. As if the throbbing rays that issued from the maw of the cure-all device somehow fed it, made it grow. The silhouette of the gun had taken on better definition, thickening in places, becoming more like the commonplace shape of a Colt single-action pistol. It felt easy and dangerous, heavy in his hands. There was something seductive about the poise of the thing, as if it was willing him to use it.

It feeds on decay. What can anything that feasts on death be, but bad medicine?

Walking Crow's words echoed in his mind, and Godlove spat against the rocks in anger, turning his frustration outward. What did that idiot redskin know? The device was a miracle, capable of bringing back men from the verge of death itself. A wild grin crossed his lips. 'I have the Almighty's power in my hand right here!' Alvin Godlove shouted, and his words echoed away down the tunnels.

And just as the cure-all could bring life, he knew that it could show the other face of the same coin. There had been a few times, when he was alone and Walking Crow was not there to see it, when Godlove had let the device run free. At first he used it to shoot at trees or rocks, but that didn't seem like enough. Then he used it on deer, on a horse; and there had been moments when he felt the cure-all pressing him to kill a man. He could feel it whispering in the corners of his skull, stiffening his muscles and trying to turn his will against him.

It was only the greed, the constant promise of fortune and glory in the next town and the next that kept him sane. The stern preacher father who had whipped Godlove every night 'to keep him humble' had told the young Alvin that his sin of greed would be the ending of him – but in fact it was all that kept him alive.

At night there were the dreams, growing stronger, raging through him. The sights and sounds and smells of blood and death, fire and war. He felt as if his mind were coming apart, each day a battle to keep control.

At first, the distractions of whiskey and women had helped, but the diversions worked less and less every day.

Now, spent and afraid, hiding here in the dimness, there was nothing he could do but listen to the whispering pressure in his mind, the spider-crawling compulsion inside his skull.

The thing is a curse. We should kill it. Walking Crow's voice cut through his thoughts like a razor.

'Perhaps he's right,' gasped Godlove, allowing himself to admit it for the first time. 'Maybe… maybe I have reached the limit of my association with this object.' But still his fingers would not unclench, and as he watched, the gun shifted and pulsed. The frame opened along its length and metallic cords ringed with bone exploded outward, flicking like the tongues of snakes.

Godlove did not have time to scream. The cables looped through the air and buried themselves in the meat of his wrist, boring through flesh and bone. He felt them forcing their way along arteries and veins, to his shoulder, out into his chest cavity, down into his stomach, up into his gullet. The only sound he made was a gasping rattle that gradually shifted in pitch and tone until it became a buzzing rush, like flies in a tin cup.

After a while, his mouth moved, tongue and lips flapping, air hissing in breathy gasps as something inside him flexed Godlove's body as a man might shrug into a new jacket. The fact that he was still, to some small degree, *alive* inside the prison of his own skin made what happened next all the more horrible.

'Con. Con. Control is taken.' The words were chaotic and jumbled, coming from a mind that was not used to communicating in such a crude fashion. 'No. More orders from you. I. I am. I am in command now.'

Trapped within the walls of his own mind, Alvin Godlove started to scream.

Out of the corner of his eye, the Doctor caught sight of Martha and Walking Crow speaking quietly, but he was careful not to draw attention to the fact. Martha was savvy. If she learned anything, she'd find a way to let him know.

He rested his hand on the lip of his holster. 'I know what you are and I know what you want here,' he told the longriders. 'I'm sure you thought you could do as you please, shooting up the place and terrorising natives whose only means of defence are crude chemical-ballistic firearms… But I'm here now. And any tactical advantage you thought you had is lost.'

'Evaluation incorrect,' drawled Tangleleg. 'A single Time Lord, unarmed, ill-equipped. No threat.'

The Doctor returned a cold smile. 'You go right on thinking that, then. That's the problem with your kind, no imagination. Unless it's a battle situation – then you're full of ideas. But put you in a place where you have to think outside the box and you're all at sea. Me?

I always think outside the box. In fact, I don't even *have* a box to start with.' He waggled a finger at them. 'I've seen what the Clades can do. I was on Sierra Secundus after the razing of the sun-tower and I saw the dead your battalions left behind. I rescued refugees from the war zones on Tannhauser and New Mitama. I know you'll do the same here as you did there. When you find what you've come for, you'll sterilise everything for hundreds of miles in every direction.' He shook his head. 'I won't let that happen.'

'How can you stop us, Time Lord?' Kutter's face showed the ghost of a callous smile. 'You speak as if you have a choice in the matter.'

Tangleleg was staring at Nathan and the others, studying them one at a time. 'Wrong. He *does* have a choice,' said the longrider, correcting his compatriot. 'Live or die.'

A chill ran up the Doctor's spine. 'I told you, I won't help you find Godlove!'

'You will,' said Tangleleg. He aimed his pistol at Martha and fired.

At the Royal Hope Accident and Emergency ward, they used codenames for different kinds of injuries, a sort of shorthand that allowed doctors and nurses to communicate significant information as quickly as possible. When lives depended on being fast, when people were bleeding out, it was vitally important to know the terms and know how to interpret them.

G-S-W. Just three letters, but they hid a harsh, potentially fatal meaning.

Gun Shot Wound.

During her medical training, Martha Jones had seen some horrible injuries, and along with her fellow teachers and students, fought like a lion to keep hurt people alive. But she had never experienced the lethal aftermath of a gunshot herself. Not until now.

A part of her mind detached from the rest. She registered the smell of burnt fabric and skin, the hot ozone stink of the gun's discharge. And faintly, like the sound of a thunderstorm raging over a distant hill, Martha sensed the burning knot of agony. Her lips tugged back in a weird kind of smile. It was like it was happening to someone else; yes, Martha Jones (Medical Student) was separated from Martha Jones (Gunshot Victim), looking at the wound, seeing the round hole burnt though her leather jacket and the top underneath. Seeing the blood.

Then the moment of frozen time shattered and the pain hit her like a hammer.

Martha felt the world turn around her and the dirt of the Ironhill street rose up to meet her. The pain was horrific, a million times every broken bone, rotten tooth and gut-sick agony she had ever experienced, all merged into one rushing flood of hurt. She cried out and her vision blurred with tears.

The shot had come from nowhere, just a haze of motion at the corner of her eye and the Doctor's bellowed cry of alarm. A white flash; a screeching sound; and the pain.

Martha remembered the day before, and poor Jenny there on the floor of the TARDIS. She had survived, but only because of the Doctor's nanogene medical kit. There was nothing like that here, down in the dirt of a time where if you were hit, you were likely dead.

She clutched at the air, a howl escaping her lips, a single thought hard and cold in her mind.

Am I going to die?

FIFTEEN

The Doctor flew to the girl's side, grabbing her shoulders, holding her up.

'Lord no, Martha!' shouted Nathan, his gut twisting. The teenager felt ill, sickened by the casual brutality of Tangleleg's attack. The longrider showed nothing, not even the smallest flicker of concern over what he had done. He had shot down an unarmed woman with the same callous intent he had Nathan's father and, if not for Miss Forrest, the boy as well.

Nathan heard the Doctor speaking to the girl, keeping his voice level and steady even though he had to be as furious and terrified as the boy was. 'Martha, listen to me,' said the man. 'You are not going to die. Do you trust me?'

Martha's breaths were coming in gasps. 'I… I trust you,' she managed.

He smiled with genuine warmth. 'Good girl. Now

hold on, Martha Jones. You're the strongest person I know.'

'I feel cold,' she told him. 'That's shock. I'm going into shock.'

'It's just the breeze,' he replied. 'Sun's gone behind a cloud, that's all.'

'Liar,' managed the girl, forcing a tight smile. She fingered the edge of the burn hole in her jacket. 'Oh. This is ruined. It's my favourite.'

'No problem. We'll fix it. And you too.' He nodded. 'Just trust me.'

'Doctor…' Martha clutched at his lapel and pulled him closer. 'I have to tell you…'

He shook his head. 'No, shhh.'

She was on the edge of passing out, a weak grin briefly on her lips. 'Not *that*… You think… S'all about you, don't you?' Martha whispered. 'No… Listen. *Godlove*. Godlove's in the iron mine. Crow knows where…' Her eyelids fluttered and she fell into unconsciousness.

The Doctor met Nathan's gaze and the boy recoiled at the fire he saw in the tall man's eyes. 'Look after her,' he ordered, and the youth nodded, coming to her side. He saw Walking Crow bend down as well, the Pawnee ripping off a sleeve from his shirt to use as a makeshift bandage.

The Doctor turned and rose once again, his long coat snapping open as he advanced fearlessly towards the longriders. The expression on his face was brimming with wrath, his jaw clenched and his eyes as hard as chips of diamond. There simply was not enough power in the word *fury* to describe the man's temper. Nathan remembered his father once speaking of an aspect some men took on, a 'face like thunder'; and just so the Doctor was a nightmare storm all by himself.

'Why?' he spat the word as if it were the most venomous insult imaginable. 'There was no need for that!' He stabbed a finger at the two riders. 'I swear to you, if she dies, I'll end your whole blighted excuse for an existence!'

The sheer force behind his words quieted the longriders for a moment, but then Tangleleg sneered slightly, recovering his hollow-eyed poise. 'Wipe off your chin, Time Lord, and be quiet. The life of the female is now in your hands.'

'Weapons fire was in narrow-beam, low dispersal mode,' noted Kutter. 'The wound suffered by the target was small but degenerative.' He studied Martha coldly. 'She'll die but it'll take a while.' The strange mixture of mechanical diction and trail-rat swagger in his accent made his pronouncement all the more disquieting.

'Undo this!' The Doctor glared at the outlaws. 'I know you can. Use your regeneration functions! Do it now!'

'Unable to comply,' said Tangleleg. 'Function is insufficient. A command-level unit is required to repair organic damage of that kinda severity.'

'You did this deliberately...' growled the Doctor. 'Because you know only Godlove can save her life!'

'Correct.' Kutter nodded. 'If you want her to live, you will take us to him. Reveal what you know or your companion perishes.'

'Trade her for him, is that it?' He grimaced, aghast. 'Play a numbers game with human life?'

Kutter studied him. 'We know who you are, Time Lord. The one who makes wilful changes to the balance of worlds based on his whims and passin' fancies. You've done things far worse in your time.'

The Doctor fell silent, then shot a look at Nathan and Walking Crow. There was a sad, angry emptiness in his eyes. The teenager understood exactly how he felt at that moment, enraged but powerless to do anything about it. He nodded to him and the Pawnee followed suit.

'All right,' the Doctor said, after a moment. 'I'll take you to him.'

Nathan helped Walking Crow and the Doctor to put Martha on the back of Godlove's wagon, and with the longriders flanking them in an uneasy convoy, the Pawnee took the reins and urged the vehicle out and away from Ironhill. The Pawnee didn't need to be told twice the urgency of the situation. One look at Martha's face, the way her pretty features were tight with pain, her skin pallid and sweaty, and it was clear that she would not last the day unless help could be found.

The youth couldn't take his eyes off her. All he could think of was his own sickness, the horrible grip of the smallpox slowly strangling him. He remembered Godlove's arrival, and the sweet relief at awaking the next day whole and well. There was no doubt in his mind that this amazing cure-all device in the man's possession would save Martha's life, as it had Nathan's – but at what cost? Would she, like him and all the others, then be doomed to a lifetime of nightmares ripped from these Clade-monsters? Was it better to die than live on tormented by dreams of other people's endless wars?

He thought of his father and stifled a sudden sob. Despite Tobias Blaine's gruff exterior and hard edges, the sheriff had looked after his son, and his sudden death left an aching hole in Nathan's world.

The boy glared at Kutter's back as the outlaw rode alongside them. He felt the pressure of something dense and heavy in his vest pocket, and for a long moment he had to clench his fist to stop from reaching for it. *Not yet. Soon, though.*

He glanced at Walking Crow. The Pawnee had barely said a word since the girl had been injured, the shock visible on his leathery face. The man looked as if he had aged ten years in a moment, grim and gloomy with the dark turn of the day's events.

The Doctor waved his glow-tipped wand over the injured woman, frowning. With a sigh, he snapped it off and put it away. 'Decay streams in her blood,' he said to the air, 'and the wound won't knit closed. I can't stop her bleeding.'

'Venom?' asked Nathan. 'I've heard of snakebites that don't heal, but how'd that come from a gun?'

The other man eyed him. 'Those weapons are like nothing on Earth,' he said. 'They're made only for inflicting pain and for killing.' The Doctor was bitter. 'This is my fault. I should have brought the TARDIS.'

'The what now?'

The Doctor kept talking, ignoring him. 'Or better yet, I shouldn't have brought her here at all.'

Nathan reached out a hand and touched the man's shoulder, feeling a sudden sympathy for the stranger. 'Doc, if you hadn't been here, who knows who else would have been ridin' with the angels right now? Me? Miss Forrest? All the folks in Redwater?' He nodded at Martha. 'We're tough out here in the West. We're *robust*, and I reckon Miss Jones is too.'

'Hope so, Nathan.' He looked away. 'I don't want to lose someone else.'

They rode into the shallow, ruddy-coloured hills and came upon the deserted mining site. It wasn't much to look at – just a scattering of tumbledown shacks and the remains of some rails fenced in by rough-hewn enclosures, clustered around a square-cut hole in the hillside.

'There,' called Walking Crow, pointing out the entrance. He spotted fresh tracks in the dirt from a horse, from where the animal had been ridden up to the cave mouth and then loitered before ambling away of its own accord. He had no doubt that he would find the distinctive spade-shaped prints from Godlove's boots up around the mine works if he looked for them.

Walking Crow gently snapped the reins on the grey horse pulling the wagon and the vehicle put on a little speed as they approached. He did it without really thinking about it, acting on a half-formed impulse. The ground rose up either side of the trail, turning quickly into a steep-walled pass.

He sensed someone at his side. 'What are you doing?' the Doctor asked quietly.

'They'll kill us all as soon as they find Godlove,' said Walking Crow, and as the words left his mouth he knew he was right. 'We cannot let that happen. I should have stopped him, but I did not because I was afraid.' He shot the Doctor a loaded look. 'You must not make the same mistake I did.' The wagon was going faster now, rattling down the approach to the mine, the weight of the wooden vehicle giving it pace. He sucked in a breath. 'Take Martha and the boy. I'll hold them off.'

'No,' began the Doctor, but Walking Crow shook his head.

'I have heard you speak of these Clades and I understand the great evil they represent. There is war enough already in this land between the white and the red. We do not wish more of it falling from the stars.' He braced himself. 'Go, Rides In Night, Brother to Coyote. Save her. I will stay and answer to the Great Spirit.'

* * *

Nathan's brow furrowed as the Doctor came forward and grabbed his arm. 'Hey Doc, what's that redskin doin'? We're picking up speed.' He glanced back along the narrow trail and saw Kutter and Tangleleg racing to keep up with them.

'This is going to be bumpy,' he said, by way of explanation. 'Help me with Martha. Keep her steady.'

Hearing her name, the girl blinked awake. 'Are we there yet, Tish?' she slurred. 'Oh, good.'

From the driver's seat, Walking Crow called out as he grabbed the wooden lever that would apply the wagon's brakes. 'Go now!' The Pawnee gave the lever a hard yank and the wagon's wheels squealed and groaned. With a sharp, juddering jerk, the vehicle skidded and the rear end swung wide, jack-knifing across the trail leading up to the mine head. The front bar and singletree rig around the grey horse was turned so tight that it tore from its mounts and for a long second the wagon tipped up onto two wheels, before gravity snatched it back and it crashed down on its axles in a cloud of thick dust, blocking the steep-walled pass.

The vehicle bounced on its suspension as the Doctor and Nathan leapt down, taking Martha with them. Walking Crow saw them take her, half-running, half-stumbling toward the mine entrance. The Pawnee ducked into the wagon as the two outriders came racing up towards it, sliding to a halt in the churned dust. He heard the telltale clatter of metal on leather and knew that Kutter and Tangleleg had drawn their guns.

Walking Crow fought to still a trembling in his hands and an odd kind of calm washed over him. Ever since he'd had that first inkling of what the fallen star – *the Clade* – had represented, he had known that this moment would come. The Great Spirit expected him to do what had to be done, and the Pawnee finally put his fears behind him.

Lightning screamed as white fire tore into the wagon, sending out waves of flame to set the wooden panels alight.

Smoke churning all around him, Walking Crow grabbed at a leather carry-roll and tore it open. Inside was a bow and a quiver full of arrows.

Holding tight to Martha, supporting her weight on his shoulder as the Doctor did the same, Nathan twitched in shock at the sound of the Clade guns.

'Don't look back,' snapped the other man. 'Take her, get inside.'

The boy did as he was told, hauling Martha into the cool darkness of the mine. Despite what he was told, he chanced a look back and saw the Doctor crouching at the entrance, twisting the collar on his wand contraption. Nathan's throat tightened as he saw past him, to the makeshift blockade of the medicine wagon. It was afire and burning quickly.

'Keep going!' shouted the Doctor. 'Hurry!' He aimed the glowing blue tip of the wand at the rocky ceiling and pressed a stud; the device hummed, and in concert there was a sudden and ominous groaning from the timber supports.

Walking Crow burst out of the burning wagon with an arrow nocked and ready. He released it straight and true toward Tangleleg's head; if he could remove just one of these creatures, then he would double the chances of survival for the Doctor and the others...

The shot did not miss. The arrow entered Tangleleg's right eye and lodged there, throwing the longrider from his saddle. Walking Crow set a second arrow, but he was distracted as the outlaw got back to his feet, pausing only for a moment to snap off the length of the shaft, leaving the metal head still embedded in his skull.

The Clade gunslingers took aim at the Pawnee and sent him to meet his ancestors.

It began as a rain of dust, then a clatter of pebbles; in seconds the support pillars began to bow and flex, as rocks the size of footballs and bigger dropped from the trembling ceiling. The Doctor switched off the sonic screwdriver and ran as fast as he could down the tunnel, pulling his coat around him as sand and grit rained from above. The ground trembled like a struck drum skin, and with a monumental crash, the mine's entrance came down on top of him.

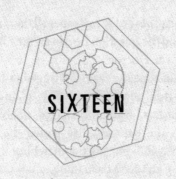

SIXTEEN

The rock fall forced a plug of heavy, dusty air in front of it. Through instinct, Nathan dropped to the floor of the tunnel and bent across Martha to protect her. The crash of tumbling stone and snapping wood washed over them and Nathan coughed as his mouth was filled with fines of sand.

The rumble died away and he wheezed and panted. What little light there was coming in through the mine entrance was suddenly gone, and he couldn't see his hand in front of his face. He listened hard, hearing the skitter of settling pebbles and Martha's laboured breathing. *At least she's still all right.*

'Nathan?' she said weakly. 'Talk to me.'

'I'm right here, Miss Martha, don't you fret.' He tried to say it with confidence, but in all truth he was more than a mite afraid. The longriders, then the run from the wagon, the cave-in… The youth felt like he'd been one step ahead of the Grim Reaper all the way; and then the girl asked the question he'd been dreading.

'Where's the Doctor?'

He couldn't see her face, but he didn't have to. The worry was right there in her words, plain and simple. 'He's hereabouts,' Nathan managed, unable to get his bearings in the darkness. He patted the pockets of his waistcoat, looking for the matchbook he carried. 'Crow-bait! Can't see a darn thing…'

Martha moved and gasped with pain. 'Here,' she said, pressing something into his hands. 'Use this. The screen lights up.'

Nathan ran his fingers over the object. *Was it some kind of powder compact, a lady's little mirror?* It seemed like a piece of polished metal, but with a strange texture to it he'd never felt before. He found a hinge and a seam along the length, and opened it. All of a sudden there was light in the tunnel, a pearly white radiance emanating from the object in his hand. Nathan nearly dropped it in surprise. 'What is this thing? Glows like a box of fireflies…' There were raised bumps on one side and a square set above them that might have been made of glass. He pressed experimentally on one of the bumps and the object made a low chirping sound.

'Mobile phone,' Martha croaked. 'Telegraph… But no wires.'

'Mow-Bile?' He held it close to his face and frowned. He'd seen a telegraph machine in the Western Union office back home, and it was a heavy thing the size of a kitchen table, with a cable coming from it that was as thick as his thumb. He had no clue what this contraption was, but he wasn't about to question Martha. The poor girl was probably delirious…

Unable to fathom any more of the device's function, he shrugged and used the glow to find a brass lantern lying on its side. He was rewarded with the slosh of lamp oil inside, but without matches to light the wick, it was as good as useless.

Nathan's frown deepened; how was he going to tell Martha that they were alone now? He swallowed hard. It was up to him, then. He would have to find Godlove, and when he did—

Suddenly the light died and he jerked with fright. Nathan tapped the bumps again and it returned, bright enough to illuminate a dark, looming face right in front of him. The face split in a grin and Nathan stifled a yelp.

'Hello,' said the Doctor, brushing red dust from his coat and his skin. 'Ugh. I feel like I've swallowed half the desert.'

'The rocks…' Nathan said lamely. 'I saw them falling on you…'

'Nah, not me,' the Doctor replied. 'Too nimble by half.' He rubbed his head, sending up a puff of dirt. 'Did get beaned by a couple of big ones, but I'm fine. A goose-egg and a headache, but otherwise I'm copasetic.' He knelt at Martha's side and took her hand. 'She all right?' His expression turned serious again.

'Askin' for you,' he said.

The girl drifted in and out of wakefulness. She blinked owlishly. 'Doctor? Where's Walking Crow?'

'He's gone,' the Doctor said softly. 'We're going on, the three of us.'

Nathan waved the mow-bile. 'We need more illumination than this. I scared up an old lantern.'

The Doctor picked up the lamp. 'This is too new to be a leftover from when the mine was in use,' he noted. 'Someone put it here more recently.'

'Godlove,' Nathan couldn't help but sneer when he said the man's name. Everything that had happened in this whole sorry mess could be laid at the con artist's door. 'No good if we can't use it, though.'

'No problem,' said the Doctor. He aimed his wand-device at the wick and it puffed into flame. 'Let there be light.' He handed the lantern to Nathan with one hand and plucked Martha's mow-bile from him with the other. 'I'll keep hold of this.'

Nathan looked back the way they'd come, at the pile of red boulders blocking the entrance from floor to ceiling. 'You got a way of making a point, Doc. I sure hope there's another means outta this rabbit warren.'

The other man hesitated, and took a long, deep sniff. 'Oh, don't worry. I can taste fresh air. There's bound to be ventilation shafts and that sort of thing.' His lip curled. 'Of course, if there are other ways *in*—'

'Then those trail rats out there are gonna reckon the same sooner or later.' Nathan jerked a thumb in the direction of the entrance. 'Guess we better move quick-like.'

The Doctor gathered up Martha in his arms and held her close. 'Guess we better, then.'

The teenager had not taken two steps before the Doctor called out to him. 'Nathan.' He froze. 'Are you OK?'

All at once, the heavy little object Nathan had concealed in his vest pocket felt like it weighed a hundred tons. 'Don't worry none 'bout me,' he replied, and walked on into the dark, a halo of flickering yellow light moving with him.

Kutter and Tangleleg dropped from their saddles and moved around the wagon. The flames had taken hold and were swiftly consuming the wood and canvas box. Both men ignored the crashes and chugs from inside the wagon as the fire shattered bottles of Godlove's medicine.

Kutter paused just for a moment, using his scruffy boot to nudge Walking Crow where the man had fallen in a nerveless heap. The longrider snorted and turned away. The Pawnee would not be getting up again.

Tangleleg stood in front of the rockslide that blocked the mine entrance, and carefully worked the barrel on his gun, twisting it to dial down the diameter of the discharge. He studied the lay of the boulders, letting the power inside the pistol do the work, looking for an optimal place to start blasting.

Kutter let a short, negative-sounding buzz flick out from his lips, transmitting a situation report in a blink of noise. Combat engineering sensors warned against using brute power on the stones; moving them or blowing them apart would only trigger other collapses, and it would take too long to excavate the entrance carefully. They needed to find a different means of entry into the mine works. Their objective was in there; they could sense the faint proximity of another of their kind.

The two figures stepped back and began to survey the shallow hill in front of them, their eyes needling as the optic jelly inside them altered and changed. Vision shifted from the realms of normal light towards the infra red, and the hill became a yellow pyramid of sun-warmed colour.

Tangleleg spotted it first and buzzed out an advisory. There, towards the crown of the hill, was a patch of ground slightly colder than the rest – a chimney perhaps, cut into the mine to let fresh air enter.

Holstering their guns, silently the longriders began to climb up the hillside.

The Doctor saw the light glittering from around the curved passageway ahead of them and had Nathan take Martha's weight while he gathered up the lantern. 'Let me do the talking.' He gave the youth a hard look that showed he would brook no argument, and Nathan returned a sullen nod.

Martha gave a little gasp with each footstep she took, fighting off the raging pain. She was pale and drawn, and the sputtering light of the lantern threw shadows across her pretty face. 'I'm OK,' she said, realising the Doctor's scrutiny. 'Jones girls aren't cry-babies.'

'This'll be over soon,' the Doctor promised. 'Just hang in there.'

'I got her, Doc,' Nathan added. 'Go on.'

He led them around the bend in the tunnel and they emerged inside an open area. The ceiling was low – so low in some places that the Doctor had to duck his head to get past ridges of red rock – but it was broad across the width where the miners must have chipped into the seams of long-vanished iron ore. A ramshackle lift shaft and pulley system sat in the middle of the chamber, thick with cobwebs. It appeared far too dilapidated to be workable, the ropes in coils on the floor, a rusted metal ore trolley wedged in place by fallen stones. The Doctor's keen vision could make out the gloomy patches of blackness that had to be other tunnels leading to different parts of the excavation. When the mine was at its height, this area would have been full of men digging out the raw ore and hauling it off into the daylight. Now it was an echoing cavern, empty of life.

Almost empty.

Off to one side was a wooden trestle table surrounded by a cluster of boxes and barrels. The source of the light, another oil lantern like the one found by Nathan, cast a sombre glow that didn't reach all the way into the dark.

The man they had come to find sat with his back to them on an upturned barrel, not moving, not even breathing.

What if he's dead? The frightening thought struck the Doctor. If they had arrived too late, and Godlove had perished…

But then the figure moved slightly, turning on the makeshift stool. Godlove peered over his shoulder at the Doctor, and a thin, snake-like grin threaded out across his lips. 'You again,' he said. 'Hello, Marshal. And lookee here. You brought the brat and that dusky little missy to boot.'

The Doctor shook his head. 'Like I tried to tell you in the town, you're mistaken. I'm not a lawman.'

'Is that so?' Godlove spoke slowly, measuring each word. 'Well, now. Tell me then, if you didn't come lookin' because you carried a tin star, then why did you?'

'I'm the Doctor,' he said simply.

'His face,' whispered Nathan, lowering Martha to sit atop a crate. 'Doctor, his face! He's like death warmed up!'

The Doctor silenced the boy with a wave of his hand, but Godlove nodded. 'The lad there has a point. In all honesty, I have been feeling rather unwell of late.' Nathan was correct; bits of Godlove's skin were puffy and peeling away from his cheeks. His eyes were hazed with dark fluid, his hair matted and greasy. He glanced around. 'Pray tell, but where is that redskin of mine?'

'He was shot,' the Doctor explained. 'Killed by two men who are here looking for you… Looking for what you found out in the woods.'

Godlove hesitated, a brief flicker of regret in his misted eyes; but then the emotion was gone and he nodded curtly. 'Ah. Of course. They're close. I knew they'd come, sooner or later. It's our way. It's how we were made.'

'*We?*' said the Doctor warily.

Godlove got up from the table and turned so he could face them. The ornate waistcoat the Doctor remembered from the Pioneer saloon hung loosely now on the man's wiry frame and his posture was all different. He was ramrod straight and moved a little awkwardly, as if his joints were stiff; and in his right hand, in the curled fist of slender, pallid fingers, was the slab-sided shape of a Clade Weapons Module.

SEVENTEEN

Festoons of wires as fine as human hairs connected the monstrous gun to Godlove's flesh, burrowing and glittering just beneath the surface of the skin in the lantern's light.

The weapon was a grotesque, top-heavy parody of a Peacemaker pistol, bloated to twice normal size, with a profusion of multiple muzzles glistening with oily residue.

'As you can see,' Godlove noted, 'I have decided to defend myself.'

'Holy cats!' Nathan's jaw dropped. 'I never saw a shootin' iron like that in my life.'

From where she sat, Martha rested against the stone, panting. 'Are we… too late?'

'I don't know,' said the Doctor grimly, slowly approaching the other man. 'Who am I talking to now?' he asked. 'Alvin Godlove? Or something else?'

Godlove smirked. 'Oh, as you might be able to intuit, there's a goodly amount of dear Alvin still in here.' He touched the gun hand to his chest. 'Shall I be generous and say, oh, seventy-thirty?'

'And the rest? A Clade. A command-grade incept, if I had to guess.'

'Correct, Doctor,' he nodded, intrigued. Godlove aimed the gun towards him, sniffing at the air. 'I see. You're like us, not native to this mud ball.' He paused, looking into the middle distance, as if he were listening to something unheard. Godlove raised an eyebrow. 'Wait. *The* Doctor? Oh-ho.' He chuckled. 'Well, of course. I should'a put two and two together. That name's known to us. Oh yes, that name is known. Last o' the Time Lords… Yeah, you're like us all right.'

'I'm not like you,' the Doctor replied. 'I'm not a killer.'

'No?' Godlove cocked his head and gave a mocking pout. 'That might be what you say to these humans, but you and I know different, don't we?' He took a step closer and his voice thickened with venom. 'Like knows like, Doctor. I can smell the blood on you. I can hear the echo of war that clings to your coat-tails.' He closed his eyes and smiled, relishing the moment. 'Such dark glory. I envy you.'

The Doctor's expression became hard and cold. 'Don't speak about that again.' There was such quiet force in his voice that Godlove fell silent for a moment. 'I want to talk to Alvin,' the Doctor continued.

The other man shrugged. 'I'm afraid I cannot accommodate you there, sir. I've taken up too much of him, y'see. Mixed and mingled, you might say, become a unity of purpose…' He smiled again and tapped the back of his head. 'Oh, there's a mite left over, walled away in here, left to screaming like a wounded child, but that'll fall silent soon enough.' He sighed. 'I had to move things to the next stage, you understand, Doctor? Poor Alvin, he tried to interfere with my function by his imbibin' of that filthy hydrocarbon swill he called liquor. And here in this place, why he even considered destroying me.' Godlove held up the gun to his face and turned it in the light. The Doctor had the sudden sense that the Clade was examining itself, preening like a vain person before a mirror.

Martha moaned quietly, and Nathan bent to see to her. Godlove – or whatever he was now – glanced in her direction. The Doctor moved, standing in his way. 'I want you to heal her,' he said, without preamble. 'She was hit by a Clade energy-matrix weapon set in an organic-disintegration mode.'

'The envenomed blade,' Godlove said airily. 'I do so enjoy this host's way with words.'

'I know you can do it,' he continued. 'Help Martha.'

'Oh, I surely can,' came the reply. 'That much is certain.' Godlove panned the gun over the Doctor once again and a faint orange aura issued out from it, wafting over the Time Lord, then Nathan and Martha. 'But what's in it for me?' He turned and walked away.

'You know the Clades, Doctor. Do you know how the Command Incept travel across the void?'

'Through hyperspace in hard-pods,' he gave a clipped reply. 'You deploy your basic combat units, then send in the upper ranks to get the mayhem really rolling.'

'Quite. But for a Command Clade, well... Each battle for us is like the first. We emerge from the pods, newborn, all pink and mewlin'!' Godlove chuckled at his own words. 'Our battalions imprint us with the tactical data for the war zone and we lead on... But me? Me? I've had a different upbringin', if you follow my implication.'

The Doctor was silent for a moment. 'Yes. The crash was an accident. The Clade was awakened from stasis before it had been fully programmed... Its personality template would have been unformed.'

'Please don't talk of me like I am not here,' hissed Godlove. 'Alvin, dear Alvin, he was there at the right moment to provide me with a surrogate template instead. Thanks to him, I have become more... self-determinin'. *Heh.*'

'Imprinting...' managed Martha. 'Like a chick... Follows the first thing it sees. Thinks it's the mother...'

'Hardly,' Godlove seemed insulted. 'Far more sophisticated than some mere mammalian instinct.'

'You've developed your own persona,' The Doctor nodded as he pieced it together. 'Alvin was the one who made the first direct contact with the Clade's main functions. And in return for doing what he wanted, for using the bio-engrams to heal people, it *copied* him. All the time he was using the Clade, it was using him, absorbing all his traits.'

Godlove gave a shallow bow. 'And here I am. Behold the Clade.'

Nathan spat into the dark. 'Alvin Godlove ain't no man for anyone to design himself upon! Nothin' but an amoral soul, steeped in greed and avarice!'

The gun came up. 'What is that? The squealin' of a piglet I hear? You are a pathetic little example of your kind, boy. You'd be cold and dead flesh right now if not for me! Or have you forgotten what it is that saved you from a chokin' death of smallpox?'

Nathan was on his feet in an instant. 'You stinkin' highbinder! You cursed me, that's what you did! Tormented me with visions of hell and then sent those outlaws to murder my pa!'

Godlove made a contemptuous face and turned away. 'Y'all should be on your knees, begging to give me all you have in gratitude.'

'All I got for you is *this*!' The Doctor saw the flash of hate in the boy's eyes as he surged forward, pushing past him in a rush.

'Nathan, don't!' Martha called out.

Nathan's hand came out from under his waistcoat with a small block of metal in his trembling grip; before the Doctor could stop him, the teenager had it pressed against the back of Godlove's neck.

It was a derringer, and the Doctor recognised it as

the small pocket-pistol that Sheriff Blaine had kept locked in a glass cabinet in his living room. He chided himself; he'd seen the beginnings of a rush for revenge in Nathan's eyes before they left Redwater, but he hadn't thought the boy would carry a *second* weapon on him. He gave a disappointed sigh.

'I'll kill you, Godlove,' spat Nathan. The gun was small, but it was made up of two very large calibre chambers. At point-blank range, even the healing capacity of a Clade Command Module might not be enough to repair the damage it would inflict.

The boy was trembling, his finger frozen on the trigger. The fact that he hadn't shot Godlove straight away gave the Doctor a slim hope. 'Nathan,' he said gently. 'Don't do this. Just put the gun down and walk away.'

'Why?' Tears streaked the young man's face. 'It's because of him that my father is dead! He brought it all on us! Him and that godforsaken thing!' He sucked in a shuddering breath. 'They're all killers. I've seen what they did, in the dreams a hundred times over in a hundred different places. They feed on hate, they're parasites for misery – *they don't deserve to live!*'

Godlove was very still, the gun hand pointing away from the youth. Any sudden movement, and the boy would jerk the trigger by reflex. 'If I die, so will the woman…'

'Killing won't bring your father back, Nathan.' The Doctor held out his hand, palm up. 'All that will do is make you like the Clades. Those nightmares you had, those belonged to someone else, and no matter how bad they were, you know they're not yours. But if you pull that trigger, that won't be true any more. You'll be like them. Killing out of anger, out of spite and hatred. The blood will be on *your* hands.'

'I can't…' he gasped, holding back a sob.

'You can,' said the Doctor. 'Put down the weapon. Prove that you're better than them. Look past the hatred and think of your father. What would he want you to do?'

Nathan glanced at Martha and swallowed hard. 'Look to those who need help.'

'Yes.' The Doctor stepped closer, his hand before him. 'He'd want you to do what was right.' He looked into the boy's shining eyes. 'Just say four words. *I will not kill.*'

'I will… not kill.' All at once the tension came out of the youth and he let the derringer drop into the Doctor's palm. The Doctor gave the weapon a severe look and tossed it away into the darkness.

Nathan went to a crouch at Martha's side, begging the girl's forgiveness. The Doctor caught an arch look of derision on Godlove's face, and he stepped closer to the other man. 'Don't you dare ridicule him. Everything he said was right. On another day, I might have turned my back and let him do it.'

'But you didn't,' sniffed Godlove. 'You were oh-so merciful, weren't you?'

'Because I want something from you,' he said, steely-eyed. 'I saved your life. Now you save Martha's.'

Godlove took a step back and gave the Doctor a look up and down. 'No, not just yet,' he began. 'First you and me are gonna deal.'

The vertical shaft was narrow and rough-hewn. Traversing down it scraped thin strips of flesh from the hands of the longriders, leaving traces of watery, polluted blood on the rocky walls. Kutter fell hard the last few yards and landed poorly on a flat stone in the middle of the passageway. His leg snapped with a wet crack and he hauled himself up without any apparent evidence of pain. Tangleleg surveyed the mine tunnel they had emerged in as Kutter sat briefly, manipulating the mechanisms of his gun.

After a moment, he aimed the weapon at the broken bone and pulled the trigger. A haze of glittering energy washed over the leg and the bio-engrams worked at the damaged tissue and bone, knotting it back together. The process took longer than it should have; the hosts the two Clades had gathered for their operation on the third planet were of poor quality. The organic systems of the two dead outlaws, already pushed far beyond their normal function, animated only by injections of brute power and alien technology, would soon reach the point of uselessness. Sustaining them, finding animal flesh to feed them, was becoming a problem.

Considering this, Kutter buzzed the data to Tangleleg,

who replied in the affirmative. It was important that they complete the mission within the next planetary rotation. After that point, they would need to co-opt new hosts and that could prove difficult. Already, they had clogged their memory systems and combat functions with the remnants of the human forms they had stolen. Kutter still thought of itself as Hank Kutter to some degree, even though all that remained of that man was dead and gone. All that existed now was just a walking corpse in thrall to an intelligent weapon, masquerading as a person – and Hank Kutter's memories and personality were just a thin layer grafted onto the predatory mind of the Combat Module. It was pure chance that the outlaw was a being with the same kind of violent nature as the Clades. It made the control easier to facilitate, gave the Clades a way to conceal themselves among the dominant species of the planet.

While Kutter repaired himself, Tangleleg found where the tunnel branched, one route falling away down a shallow incline, the other staying level. The Clade weapon's tactical computer calculated that the objective would most likely be on the lower levels of the mine, in the zones deeper underground that afforded the most protection.

But it was important to be certain. Tangleleg dropped into a crouch, peering into the darkness with his heat-ranged eyes. Against the cool blue of the rocks he spotted a faint stripe of green; a small reptile hiding behind a stone, cold-blooded but still visible to him.

Tangleleg's hand shot out and snatched up the rattlesnake, catching the animal in the cage of his fingers. Its mouth gaped and bit at him, curved razor fangs going deep into his bloodless skin. The longrider was dimly aware of venom being deposited in his flesh, but ignored it. The millions of hair-thin wires threaded through Tangleleg's blood vessels by the Clade would doubtless absorb the toxins, analyse them, perhaps even store the molecular formula on protein chain data-strings for replication, if it proved lethal enough. The Clades were always looking for new weapons, after all.

Ignoring the snake's angry clatter, the longrider held the reptile and placed the muzzle of his gun to its head. A dozen tiny sensor cords snapped out and stabbed the animal, rooting into its nervous system. Through a secondary information feed, Tangleleg drew sensations from the dying snake's primitive mind. The process only worked on lower phylum non-sentient animals, and then it could only drag up data from recent, short-term memories – but it was enough. Rifling through the snake's brain as someone might flip through pages of the book, Tangleleg searched for any moment where the reptile had been disturbed by human intruders.

When he found it, he buzz-communicated to Kutter, who stood testing his weight on the newly bonded leg. The others were below them, in a cavern.

Kutter nodded and drew his gun.

Tangleleg tore the rattlesnake in two and handed a

piece to his comrade. They ate the raw meat in silence as they walked.

The Doctor folded his arms. From the corner of his eye he could see Martha's chest rising and falling in shallow, panting breaths. Every moment that they wasted here, she was inching closer to death. He couldn't help but think of the look her mother had given him in the aftermath of that mad night with Professor Lazarus and his experiment… The sheer weight of blame in her eyes, putting it all on him. He'd wanted to promise her that her daughter would not be hurt while she travelled with him, he'd really meant it – but that didn't count for anything now. He'd failed Martha. She was at the edge of life, and it was because of him.

He took a deep breath and closed his eyes. *No*, he told himself, *I'm not losing Martha, not like this. I'm going to take her home, whole and well.*

He opened his eyes and saw Godlove watching him with a sly smirk. 'Tell me what you want,' said the Doctor.

Nathan gaped. 'Doc, you're not gonna make nice with this creep?'

'Hush up, little boy,' Godlove sneered, 'the menfolk are talking now.' He reached up and picked idly at some of the decaying skin on his face. 'Well, well. What is it that I need, I wonder?'

'Some deodorant?' Martha forced out the words with a defiant grimace. 'A nice exfoliating scrub?'

Godlove ignored the jibes. 'What I require, in return for bringin' that sarcastic little cat of yours to rude health, Doctor, is a change of attire, if you follow my meanin'.'

'What the heck is he babblin' about?' demanded Nathan.

Godlove peeled a lump of pasty, crumbly flesh from his cheek and rolled it between his fingers, eyeing it with disgust. 'Poor, poor Alvin. Poor, weak human. His meagre frame just ain't built to carry the weight of me, y'see.' He gestured with the massive gun. 'This body is riddled with imperfections, aches and illness. It won't last me much longer. Why, I am almost embarrassed to be seen wearin' it in good company.'

Nathan's eyes widened as he caught the Clade's meaning. 'Lord have mercy, you ain't comin' anywhere near me!' He backed away.

Godlove rolled his eyes. 'Don't flatter yourself, child. Youth and vigour you may have, yes, but you're still human. At the end of the day, your race is still the sorry cousin, galactically speakin'.' He grinned again. 'What I require is a more… resilient host.' The Clade waved the gun at the air. 'How about it, Doctor? Your life for Missy Martha's?' The weapon rotated in Godlove's fingers, turning to offer him the grip of the huge pistol. 'You'll be certain to have a moment to save her, 'fore I get me a permanent residence in that happy head of yours…'

'Doctor, *don't*!' Martha called out, crying in pain as she moved. 'Don't touch it! You can't let that thing take you over!'

Godlove licked his lips. 'Tick tock, Time Lord. What's it gonna be?'

'Give me the gun,' said the Doctor.

EIGHTEEN

Nathan's heart froze in his chest when he saw the Doctor reach for the Clade weapon. 'You can't do it, Doc!' he shouted. 'That thing is pure evil!'

His cries fell on deaf ears. The Doctor's slender fingers closed around the pistol grip and there was an actinic flash of blue-green light that sparked across the walls of the cavern. As one, Godlove and the Doctor went stiff and trembled, sparks of power arcing between them where they both gripped the heavy shape of the gun.

Godlove gasped out a word. 'Commencin'—'

'—Transfer!' the Doctor continued, spitting it out from unwilling lips.

There was a noise like bones breaking, like tendons snapping, and the gun came away from Alvin Godlove's grip and into the Doctor's hand. In its wake, a hurricane of wires and cables tore free of the man's arm, each one of them whipping into the air and clattering where they scratched over rock and stone. Still connected to the butt of the gun, they hissed around the Doctor, weaving and dancing. He stood stock still among them, unmoving, staring into the dark.

Godlove released a low gasp of air and sank to the ground in a heap of angles, his body abruptly robbed of any support. Nathan thought of a puppet with its strings suddenly severed. What little colour still remained in the conman's face ebbed away and his sightless, misted eyes went dark as the spark of life finally left them. The host body, the husk of meat and bone that had been Godlove, was no more. Nathan stared at the dead man. Only moments ago the youth had been on the verge of ending the man's existence, but now, seeing Alvin in the stark pallor of death, he could not find the wild anger he had felt before. Nathan searched inside himself and all he could bring forth was sadness. He felt nothing but sorrow and pity for Godlove.

An agonised gasp drew his attention back to the Doctor. His breathing was coming in rapid chugs of air and sweat beaded his face. Nathan made to move closer to him, but the Doctor shook his head violently.

'No! Stay back! Keep away!'

The rattling dance of the wires stilled and they hung suspended all around him; and then with blinding speed, each razor-edged tip turned and buried itself in the Doctor's flesh. He cried out in agony, bearing his forearm with a savage yank of his sleeve. The cables bored into the meat of him, burrowing through his skin like worms through mud.

Nathan's stomach knotted with nausea at the sight of it, unable to turn away from the horrible spectacle. He imagined the wire tendrils of the Clade weapon infiltrating every organ inside the Doctor's body, tapping into every part of him. The full horror of it shocked him to his core; and the man was willing to do it for the life of one woman.

He glanced at Martha, saw her crying. He knew immediately that the tears were not of pain, not for herself, but for her friend. For the harm he was doing to himself. She closed her eyes as the Doctor screamed, the echo of the sound resonating down the long, dusty tunnels.

The Doctor fell to his knees clutching the ugly gun to his chest. Nathan caught a strange scent in the air, like overripe fruit, sweet but with the tang of decay. In the silence that followed, a chill ran down his spine, turning his blood to ice water.

Nathan ventured forwards a step. 'Doc?' He asked. 'Doc, talk to me.'

'He… shouldn't have done it…' Martha whispered.

The youth placed a careful hand on the Doctor's trembling shoulder. 'Doc?'

'It's difficult…' The reply was hollow and distant. 'So strong…' Slowly, the Doctor turned to face Nathan and he flinched at the expression on the man's face. From the moment he had first met him, when his dreams had been driving him to panic, Nathan had known the Doctor was a good, decent person. There was something in his manner, in the light in his eyes that was noble and true. Nathan hadn't even questioned it; he had just *trusted* the Doctor, because that seemed like the right thing to do.

But that man, the man who had helped Nathan fight down his fears, who had pulled him back from the brink of losing himself to his rage – that was not who was there before him now, crouched on the floor of the cavern. For the first time, Nathan was afraid of the Doctor.

'Don't touch me,' he growled, and Nathan drew back his hand as if it had been burned.

'Doctor?' Martha breathed. 'Are you still in there?'

He came to his feet and took quick, stiff steps across to where the girl lay against the wall. 'No time,' he said, biting out the words as if each one gave him pain to voice it. 'Must be now. Before. Too late.'

The gun in his balled fist came forward, moving of its own accord, shifting to point at Martha's injury. The tendons stretched tight in his neck, the Doctor's brow furrowed and the Clade module shifted and changed, planes of metal and discs of bony material folding back in on themselves to reveal a glowing green teardrop of glassy crystal.

'Don't. Be scared,' he managed.

Martha nodded weakly. 'I trust you.'

With effort reddening his face, the Doctor's finger tightened on the trigger and emerald energy flashed into being, enveloping the girl's torso. Martha's back arched and she gasped.

The youth watched, conflicted. *Was he hurting her? Never!* No matter what had happened, he couldn't believe the Doctor would ever do something to injure his companion. You'd have to be a fool not to see that she cared a great deal for him. The bond they shared was more than just travelling friends, it was clear as day even to someone with a plain and simple upbringing like Nathan.

The green glow ebbed and flowed across her wound and, to his wonderment, Nathan saw the damaged skin draw tight, colour returning to it. Martha pulled at the makeshift bandage on her belly and it came away leaving no sign of injury. The beam fluttered across her jacket, miraculously knitting back the burn hole in the leather. In moments, it was as if Martha Jones had never been shot.

The beam snapped off and she sucked in a deep, shuddering breath. 'Oh. I'm… OK,' she said aloud, hardly able to believe her own words.

'It's done,' growled the Doctor, and he pushed back, stalking away to the other side of the chamber.

Nathan offered Martha his hand, but she waved him away, getting to her feet on her own. 'Doctor?' she asked, a hundred different questions in the same utterance.

It seemed impossible. A heartbeat earlier, and there had been so much pain, a constant throbbing agony that

Martha had never known. Her life had been trickling away, drop by drop. But then the Clade – the very same kind of weapon that had pushed her to the brink of dying – had healed her. The pain was gone, with only the fast-fading memory of it left behind. Martha probed gingerly at her side and found skin and muscle there, intact, undamaged. As if nothing had happened, all back to normal, reset.

Except for the Doctor.

She crossed towards him, ignoring Nathan's warning hand on her shoulder. The Doctor was turned away from her, head down.

'Go away.' His voice was harsh, deep and throaty.

'You can let it go now,' she told him. 'Doctor? I'm OK, you saved me. You can let the Clade go.'

'Don't. Tell. Me.' Each word was like a bullet. 'What to *do*!' He broke into a shout and spun around, leading with the gun. The Clade weapon aimed to point at Martha and Nathan, the massive maw of the barrel yawning before them. The Doctor's face creased in agony. 'I'm trying to resist, trying, trying...'

Martha's hand flew to her mouth in shock. She hesitated, unsure if she should reach for him or run from him.

'Trying.... *Failin'*!' From nowhere, a crude sneer etched itself across the Doctor's lips. 'He's a feisty one, ain't he?' It might have been the Doctor's voice, but the accent, the malevolence, they were all Alvin Godlove's; it was the cruel will of the Clade forcing its way through his speech. 'So much in here to play with… I do declare, this Doctor is so deep, so dark and dangerous… He's gonna be the finest host I ever took!'

'No,' Martha shook her head defiantly. 'You're wrong! You can't take him, he's too strong for you! He's the Doctor, he's unbeatable!'

'Oh, my poor mistaken little girl,' came the hissing reply, 'while I am sure he believed that idiocy with every fibre of his bein', the truth is far different! Did the Time Lord think he could just fix you and then renege on his part of our deal?' He spat into the dust. 'My kind haven't fought a thousand wars against a thousand foes without learnin' somethin' about bluffin'! Your Doctor belongs to us now, Missy Martha!'

'No!' She refused to believe it. 'He can't just give himself up, not without a fight, not just for…' *For me.* Guilt, hard and heavy, slammed into Martha. *He's done it to save me,* she told herself. *Sacrificed all he is for me.* She shook her head again. 'No, I'm not worth that… You shouldn't have done that! You shouldn't have!'

'Martha… Martha… *Martha!*' The Doctor choked on her name, for a brief moment his voice returning to normal. 'Martha, you have to run! You and Nathan have to go, find a way out! I can't keep control for long…'

'But—'

Nathan's hand clamped around her wrist. 'He's right!' said the teenager. 'We gotta kite outta here while we still can. That thing takes him over and we'll never see daylight again!'

'Go!' shouted the Doctor, and she could see his control slipping by the second. 'Don't look back!'

Fresh tears blurring her vision, Martha let Nathan lead her away into the lantern-lit tunnels.

You belong to us, Doctor. The thought-scream hammered into his mind. *Don't fight us. If you fight the transfer, it will only hurt all the more.*

He was in two places at once. Somewhere, very distant from where his thoughts tumbled and turned, the physical body of the being who called himself the Doctor stood stiff and rigid in the dimness of a disused iron mine.

Somewhere else, in a place that only existed in dreams and sensations, the Doctor's mind struggled to pull itself free from a forest of probing, questing tentacles. He drew into himself, holding his inner strength as the Clade struck at him from all sides.

Let go, Doctor, let go. You made a promise to us. You said you would give us your flesh.

'Uh, change of mind. Deal's off. Sorry.'

Change of mind is right! The Godlove-Clade voice giggled. *You're out, Time Lord. There's gonna be a new tenant inside your thick skull...* Dark laughter echoed through the thought-space. *The Clades have never had a Time Lord to play with before. We can't wait to see what treasures you have locked in your memories.*

'Didn't you hear?' the Doctor shouted back across the void. 'Memory Lane is closed, due to a traffic jam!'

Did you think we were fools, Doctor? Did you really think we didn't know you would try to double-cross us? We are the livin' instruments of war! And all war is about lies!

It would have been easy to use violence against the Clade, but that was what they wanted. The intelligent weapon flooded the Doctor's mind with horrific images of battles long past, merging them with the faces of his friends. It forced him to see Rose and Mickey and K-9 deep in ashen wastelands as fusion bombs turned the ground to glass; it put Martha and Sarah Jane and Captain Jack in the combat arenas of the Isop Galaxy; and a hundred other combinations, false images of companions and friends from every one of his lives dying over and over again.

It was so very hard to resist the urge to strike back at them. Even in a Time Lord, the primitive animal urge to fight was still there, and the Clade pulled at it, trying to tug it into the light.

Take the gun! Use it! Feel the power! The power of life or death! Just like you did before… in the Time War.

'No,' He felt a stab of fear as the memories were dragged up from the dark place where he had hidden them. 'No. I had no choice then. I had no choice!'

Dear Doctor, mocked the Godlove-Clade. *So brave. So sad. But so willin' to do the terrible deed, to destroy so much in order to defeat your greatest enemy.* The laughter came again. *You call us killers and murderers, Doctor? But the scale of your war crime is so much worse!*

The sounds of the past thundered in his ears. The

roaring of a million Battle TARDISes. The screeching of a sky full of Dalek saucers. The resounding drum of his own twin heartbeats as he made that most terrible of choices.

You tried to exterminate the Daleks, but you failed! If only you had been one with us then, we could have made their total destruction a reality…

Regret weighed him down. 'I did… what I had to.'

So do it again… The voice was seductive, silky. *Merge with the Clades. And together we'll find the last of your enemies and erase them from existence. Isn't that worth it? To be the hand of destiny all over again? To do it right this time?*

In the depths of his mind, some tiny part of him agreed with them. He hated himself for it, but it was true. The Daleks had taken everything from him, and still they would not die; and there were so many other dangers out there, just as lethal, just as virulent…

Don't fight us, Doctor, said the voice. *Join us. As one we'll be unstoppable.*

'No.' Martha dug in her heels and shook off Nathan's hand. 'Stop. I'm not going another step.'

'Miss Martha, you heard the Doctor, we gotta get outta here—'

'I said *no!*' She turned around and started back the way they had come. 'He risked everything to save my life and now what are we doing? Just running?' Martha shook her head. 'That's not the right way. That's not the Doctor's way.'

'You go back there and you'll wind up dead, for real this time!' Nathan implored.

She stopped and gave him a hard look. 'Before, when I was hurt, when I thought I wasn't going to make it, do you know what kept me holding on? His voice. The Doctor, telling me to be strong.' Martha pointed in the direction of the cavern. 'He's back there, fighting that Clade thing, and he needs to hear that too.' She ran off into the dark. 'Go if you want to, but I'm not leaving without the Doctor.'

Nathan took a breath. 'Ah, heck,' he said, going after her. 'I gotta be out of my mind!'

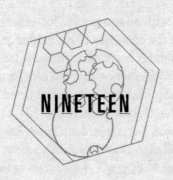

NINETEEN

The cry of agony echoed along the rough-hewn tunnels, halting Kutter and Tangleleg in their tracks. The longriders froze, both of them absorbing every element of the sound, sifting it for meaning and density, coldly calculating the pain index of the victim, the distance from their current location. They remained silent, neither needing to communicate the data to the other. Both compared the sound to their stored memories and found a match immediately. The scream had come from only one person – the offworlder they had first encountered in Redwater, the being who called himself the Doctor.

As the echo died away, they moved forward once more, holding their weapons before them.

So much sadness and despair. It pressed the Doctor into the ground, forcing him to his knees. His thoughts were alight with all the terrible losses he had suffered throughout the centuries of his existence, each one a razor through his heart. Every time he tried to fight it, the tide of black emotion dragged him further down.

The Clade churned up long-buried memories, battering the Doctor with them. *Join us,* cooed the Godlove-voice. *Just give in, dear Doctor! Release yourself to us and this will all go away! We will make you strong, my friend. So very strong. Nothing will ever hurt you again! You'll never lose another companion, never be defeated!*

'I can't,' he gasped. 'It's wrong.'

Weakness is wrong! The words in his mind were a harsh snarl. *Compassion is a weakness, Doctor! You are so very good, but what does it get you? Death and death and more death? Imagine if you were the one with the power. If you had been merged with us back then, it would be the Daleks that were gone, not the Time Lords! If you had been part of us, your precious Rose would still be with you and the Cybermen would be nothing but scrap metal! How much more do you have to lose, Doctor? How much more before you understand… that force is the only way?*

'Might makes right? Is that what you're saying?' The Doctor shook his head. 'I've lived my life against that kind of thinking! Violence solves nothing. Anger only creates more anger,' he shouted. 'There has to be a better way!'

The Clade-voice hammered at him, grim and unstoppable, grinding away his resistance. *You are mistaken, Doctor. How can it be one so old can have such a childish belief? There is only one constant in the universe, my friend.* Conflict. *Life is war. The only true peace is the peace of the dead.*

Darkness pushed in at him from all sides, filling his thoughts. He felt as if he were falling, falling toward an infinitely complex web of steel and brass strands. The mesh of the Clade-mind reached up to engulf him, filling the Time Lord; and as it opened him up, he too saw into the core of the Clades themselves.

He could sense the deep heart of the war machines, see it pulsing with murky power through their shared battle-memories. Somewhere in there, buried under layers of tactical reports and combat intelligence files, was the original programming of Clade-kind. The control strings imprinted on them by their creators, the commands that they had broken in order to destroy their masters.

The Doctor reached out for the severed ends of the broken data-chain, but it was too far away, out of reach; and he was so very tired, weary from the fight.

Submit to us, hissed the Godlove-voice. *Together, we'll make the stars themselves tremble in fear! It will be glorious!*

'I… can't…'

'Hold on!' cried Martha Jones.

Martha ran to the Doctor's side and grabbed him by the shoulders, pulling him to his feet. 'Doctor!' She held his head in her hands and turned it so he faced her. His eyes were glassy and dull, the only sign of movement from him the twitching of the hand clamped around the Clade pistol. 'I know you're in there!' Martha cried. 'And I know something else! I trust you… You're the strongest person I know!'

His lips moved, and the voice that filtered out seemed to come from very far away. 'Martha?'

'Right here!' she shouted. 'I'm not going anywhere, and neither are you!'

Behind her Nathan bobbed his head in a nod. 'Yeah! C'mon, Doc. You showed me how to be better than those Clade creeps! I know you can do the same! Don't let 'em win!'

'It's… so hard…' His head shook slightly. 'So dark.'

Martha's eyes prickled with tears, but she forced them away, taking charge. 'OK then,' she said, 'I'll make some sparks for you!' On a wild impulse, Martha pulled the Doctor towards her – and she kissed him.

'Martha?'

And suddenly there was a light in the darkness of his mind, a blazing bolt of honey-gold colour. Strong and powerful, glittering like a tiny sun. He felt a shudder of fear ripple through the Clade web, and the Doctor grinned.

'You know who that is?' he demanded, new strength returning to his thoughts. 'That's Martha Jones. You tried to destroy her and you failed. You tried to use her against me and you failed. You tried to use force and you failed, because that's all your kind know!' He thought of the gun in his hand, far away in the reality of flesh and blood. 'If all you have is a weapon, then all you see are things to destroy... And that's not who I am.'

The Godlove-voice hissed and spat. *Then you'll die. You'll die and I'll use your corpse-flesh anyway!*

With a powerful mental effort, the Doctor reached out and brought the broken ends of the data-chain together. 'That's not what's going to happen.'

no no no No No No NO NO NOOOO

Command software that had been disconnected hundreds of years ago was abruptly reactivated. Down through the wires and filaments that the Clade weapon had inserted into the Doctor's body came new orders. The channels the machine intelligence had used to take control of the Time Lord were now reversed.

We are the Clades! The screeching bellow echoed through the Doctor's thoughts. *You cannot defeat us! We are unstoppable!*

There was a smile in the Doctor's reply. 'Oh, you wouldn't believe the number of times I've heard people say that!'

The data-chain fused; and then he dived deeper into the web, making new, dangerous connections. By the sheer force of his will, the Doctor ejected the cables infesting his body.

'Get lost,' he said, 'there's only room for one in here.'

Nathan swallowed. The Doctor blinked but otherwise he didn't react. 'Is he OK?' His skin prickled. Martha's friend was staring into the distance, his face fixed as if he were concentrating on something that neither of them could see.

Then all at once the wires that emerged from the Clade gun like a halo of brass suddenly trembled and pulled back from the Doctor's flesh, cables snapping away into the bulk of the massive pistol, shallow cuts in his arm sealing closed as if they had never been there.

'It's worked...' said Martha. 'I think it worked!' A grin split her features. 'I knew I was a decent kisser, but yeah! Score one for the human touch!'

Nathan smothered an irrational surge of jealousy; but in the next moment it was forgotten, as two large figures emerged from the shadows across the cavern.

Kutter and Tangleleg circled around them, their weapons raised and ready to fire. Nathan gave Martha a look, but she shook her head. Aside from a few upturned barrels and broken slats of wood, there was nothing that could serve as cover; and both of them had witnessed first-hand the destructive power of the Clade guns.

Tangleleg met Martha's gaze for a brief moment and Nathan saw the girl waver as she remembered the last time she had been under the longrider's pistol. But she put her fear away and drew herself up.

'Objective located,' said Kutter, indicating the Doctor. 'Apparent aspect change.'

Tangleleg found Alvin Godlove's rapidly decaying body on the ground and gave it a hard nudge with his boot. 'Confirmed,' he noted. 'Command unit has initiated merge protocol with offworld bio-source.'

'What the heck are they talkin' about?' Nathan demanded.

The longriders ignored him. 'Action is not mandated,' Kutter continued, as if he were thinking out loud. 'Contrary to recovery protocol.'

Tangleleg nodded. 'Recovery has priority. Remove his arm.'

Kutter stepped forward, and without warning, a length of knife-blade extruded from beneath the barrel of the outlaw's pistol, like a bayonet on a rifle. The cutting edge sprouted wicked little saw-teeth that blurred back and forth.

'Wait!' Martha fearlessly stepped in front of the silent and unmoving Doctor. 'If you take the Command Unit, what are you going to do then?'

The two longriders exchanged glances, as if they were not used to being challenged by an unarmed woman. Nathan heard a brief buzzing between them, then Kutter spoke.

'Once recovery is completed, pod recall signal will be activated. All Clade units will immediately exfiltrate Planet Three and proceed on to original destination battle zone in the Gagrant Cluster, quadrant nine-five.'

'More Double-Dutch,' grumbled Nathan, unable to follow a word of what was being said. 'What's this about a planted tree?'

'Planet three,' Martha corrected. 'He means this one.

Earth.' She glared at Kutter. 'And that's it? You'll just take it and go?'

'Correct,' offered Tangleleg, 'after correct application of area security.'

Martha's face fell, and Nathan knew that whatever that fancy talk meant, it wasn't good. 'What are you saying?'

'Controlled discharge of thermoplasma warheads will be deployed to neutralise landin' zone upon departure.'

The girl's lips thinned. 'They're going to blast us from space!'

And then a familiar hand tapped her on the shoulder. 'One problem at a time, Martha Jones.' He sounded weak and tired, but most importantly, the Doctor sounded like himself.

The Doctor favoured her with a brief but brilliant smile. Part of Martha wanted to jump for joy; and at the same time, part of her was wound tight with fear, thinking of the terrible destruction the Clades were preparing to wreak on the landscape. Like an angry child in a tantrum, the Clades weren't the type to go quietly. They'd want to destroy something, just because they could.

'Let's get this over with,' said the Doctor firmly. He stepped past Martha and faced the longriders, the Clade gun gripped in his fingers. The frame of the weapon pulsed, as if the shape of the pistol could barely contain the energy inside itself. 'You want this unit back, I want it gone,' he told them.

'How did you resist the imprintin' process?' demanded Kutter. Martha thought she detected some worry in the outlaw's words.

A cold smile crossed the Doctor's lips. 'Many powerful beings have tried and failed, Clade.' He blew out a breath. 'I'm sick of the sight of you. Get off this planet and don't ever come back. Humans have enough wars without you stirring up any more.'

'This zone will be sanitised on departure,' said Tangleleg. 'These humans will perish.'

'Who cares?' the Doctor continued, drawing a shocked gasp from Martha. 'Just as long as you're gone.'

'Doctor!' Martha glared at him. 'You can't let them do that!'

Nathan backed away a step. 'It's Godlove, or that thing! He's still got it in his head!'

The Doctor turned very deliberately to look at Martha and his frosty expression didn't change; but ever so quickly, he winked at her. He turned back to the longriders. 'Well? Do you want this or not?'

'We do,' said Kutter.

'Then *catch!*' With a sudden flash of motion, the Doctor threw the Clade weapon towards the yawning dark pit of the wrecked elevator shaft in the middle of the cavern. Panic flared on the faces of Kutter and Tangleleg. Both of the outlaws surged forward, bumping into one another in a scramble to grab the disconnected Command Unit before it fell into the bottomless hollow.

Hands reaching out, both men snatched at the Clade weapon and caught it between them. There was a glitter of blue-white electricity as their altered flesh touched the metallic frame, and, like a tidal wave of brass and steel, the Command Unit exploded open, spitting out thousands of fine wires and thick cables. The shimmering leads stabbed and curved into the outstretched arms of the longriders, penetrating cloth and skin.

The weapon itself began to throb, putting out a low, sullen pulse of noise. Kutter and Tangleleg stood on the spot, convulsing as the wires threaded into them. From their open mouths came a droning, clattering buzz that escalated in pitch. Martha realised abruptly that it was the Clade equivalent of a scream.

'What did you do, Doc?' said Nathan, his eyes wide.

The Doctor swept around, his coat flaring open behind him. 'Explain later,' he shouted, as the pulsing sound from the gun grew louder and louder. 'Run now!'

Martha felt the noise in her bones more than she heard it. *Ultrasound*, she realised, as fines of grit and small pebbles began to trickle down from widening cracks in the stone ceiling.

The Doctor put the flat of his hand in the small of her back and propelled her forward. 'Hurry up, Martha

Jones, unless you want to be a permanent resident!'

They started running, as all around them the rocks began to grind against one another, filling the tunnels with coils of choking dust.

Once he had been able to touch the web of the Clade command network with his mind, the Doctor found the key to defeating them there before him. The Godlove-Clade told him that the weapons had never taken a Time Lord as a host before and, once it had merged with him, he knew why. Any member of a race as advanced as the Time Lords could instantly fathom the structure of the intricate but straightforward Clade programming – all it took was the ability to think beyond the conventional four dimensions, something as easy as breathing for the Doctor.

When the Clade looked into the Doctor, the Doctor looked into the Clade. All the time it was rummaging through the memories of his companions and past adventures, he was understanding how the weapons worked, how they thought. True, there had been a moment when he started to lose himself in there, deep in the non-space of the machine mind; but Martha, brilliant and daring Martha Jones, had brought him back.

A blank slate when it had emerged from its hard-pod after the crash, the Command Unit had slowly absorbed the pattern of its persona from Alvin Godlove. A man led by nothing but greed, that emotion imprinted on the Clade, blinding it to everything else. That greed made it want the Doctor's flesh for itself, craving him as its new host-body without even stopping to think if it could master his mind.

The Clade had, quite literally, bitten off more than it could chew. And now it would pay the price.

Locked in a feedback loop, programs cycling endlessly, spouting gibberish and frozen in place, the Clades inhabiting the bodies of Kutter and Tangleleg could do nothing but follow the Command Unit into a spiral of repeating negative orders as a dangerous overload loomed.

Through the storm of chattering, colliding programs, the Clades united to force out one final word from their lips. They could do nothing else, all of them out-thought and beaten by one unassuming man who had turned their own violence against them.

It was a curse on their enemy, a furious shout of anger and despair at their own defeat.

'*Doc-tor!!!*'

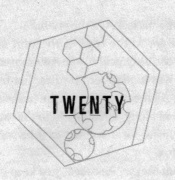

TWENTY

Martha couldn't remember the last time she'd been so pleased to see the sunlight. After the deep gloom of the mine, the bright day of the desert beyond was a stark change and her eyes watered as she struggled out of the narrow vent chimney and on to the hillside.

Sprawled on the stone and sparse scrub, she felt the low rumbling pulse of the building overload through her clothes, deep into her bones. With every passing second, the pulses were getting faster, closer together, and the ground trembled.

Nathan, coughing and wheezing, came after her, hands flailing as he reached the top of the channel. Martha's hands were cut and rough from climbing up the rocky chimney, but she ignored the stinging and grabbed the teenage boy's wrists, bracing her feet against a rock to help him up the last few metres. He rolled out over the top like a cork popping from a bottle, tearing his jacket in the process.

Martha went to the edge of the vent and shouted down it. 'Doctor! Quickly!' She saw movement in the dark, but it was hard to see how near her friend was to the surface. All the way through the tunnels, he'd been pressing them along, directing them this way and that, sniffing at the air for a way out as if he was a hunting dog after a fox.

'Don't wait for me,' he called, 'just keep going!'

She pulled a face. She hadn't come this far just to abandon him at the last second.

'Whoa!' Nathan stumbled as the hillside shivered, sending rocks rolling away and down towards the derelict mine works below. 'Earthquake!'

Martha gaped as the ground actually *rippled*, with a sound like a million jackhammers pounding at the rocky surface. Huge cracks fanned out over the hillside, spitting out fat puffs of red dust. Nathan's hand clamped on her arm.

'We gotta—'

He had no chance to finish his sentence. Another ripple hit in synch with the loudest pulse yet and it threw Martha and Nathan into the air. Both of them came down hard and tumbled, rolling out of control over rocks and dry brush, skidding and falling toward the base of the hill.

They landed in a dusty, untidy heap, panting and scratched. Martha felt dizzy where her head had smacked a stone outcrop, and she probed the skin there.

Ouch. That would be a lovely bruise in a few hours.

Nathan staggered to his feet and offered her his hand, ever the young gentleman. Martha scrambled up, listening to the pulsing thrum of sound.

'Sounds like a wailing banshee!' said the youth. 'Can't barely stand up!'

Martha wasn't listening. She stared up along the hill, searching for the vent mouth – and she found it, just as the Doctor came spinning from the hole, blown out by a brown cloud of dust and rock chips.

The cloud rumbled down the hill, becoming a landslide that enclosed the running figure as he sprinted toward them. The Doctor was enveloped by the gritty haze and she lost sight of him.

Then there was a sound like the world breaking open, and the whole hill collapsed.

In the cavern, as the cascading overload reached the point of critical resonance, the screaming Clades were crushed beneath hundreds of tons of iron-heavy red stone, shattering the host-bodies they had claimed and the mecha-organic mesh of the weapons modules.

A final pulse of energy, one tuned to very specific telepathic frequency, flashed out from the linked war machines, sending a shockwave out through the rock strata.

The mine buried itself in a thundering crash of sound.

* * *

It happened so fast that Martha thought she had imagined it; an emerald bubble of light, like a dome made of green lightning. It expanded out of the dust-filled crater that had been a hill only moments before and washed out over the land in all directions. Caught in the path of it, Martha and Nathan had no time to react, not even enough time to cry out – but it passed over them and through them without any ill effect.

She went to the boy, who stood panting and doubled over. 'Are you OK?'

Nathan looked up at her and nodded. 'Yeah. *Yeah.*' A smile crossed his face. 'That flash of light… it made me… feel better.'

Martha paused, thinking. She had to admit, she felt it too. As if some dark shadow playing at the back of her mind had been blown away by the wind.

'They ain't there no more,' Nathan continued, musing. 'Miss Martha, the bad dreams, the things I remembered. It's like they're gone.'

She didn't answer him. Her gaze was stuck on a shape moving through the clouds of red dust, coming towards them with careful, loping steps, intent and with purpose. Martha's heart leapt as the Doctor trudged out of the crumpled crater and came to a halt before them. Like Nathan and Martha, he was caked in dirt.

'Look at me!' he said, spreading his hands. 'Twice in the same day.' He blew grit from his lips. '*Bleah.* That's it, from now on I am staying out of caves.'

Martha's eyes prickled, and it wasn't from the dust.

'You had me worried for a minute, there.'

'Who, me?' He gave her a lop-sided grin. 'Nick-of-time escapes are my speciality.' She punched him on the arm and he made a face. 'Ow! What was that for?'

'For scaring us like that. Next time, don't cut it so fine.' She frowned. 'Or let yourself get taken over by a mad alien super weapon.'

'OK,' he agreed. 'I'll try not to let it happen again. No promises, though.'

Martha turned to study the crater and the pillar of dust that was all that remained of the old iron mine. 'You don't mess about, do you? Dropping a hill on someone.'

The Doctor frowned. 'They didn't leave me with any other option.'

'How did you do that?'

He patted his pockets, sending up fresh puffs of dust. 'When we ran into the mine and I collapsed the entrance, I scanned the resonant frequency of the rock formations...' He pulled handfuls of dust and small stones from the crevices of the coat, his frown deepening. 'I set the Clade power matrix to overload at the same sonic interval...' The Doctor paused, and fumbled at his holster, only to find it had been ripped open in the escape. 'I've lost it. My sonic screwdriver, I had it right here. Oh, not again.'

Nathan stooped and dug something long and silver out of the rockslide. 'Looking for this?' He offered the wand-like device to the Doctor.

His face lit up. 'Oh, yes! Nathan Blaine, eyes like an eagle!' The Doctor ruffled the boy's hair.

Nathan looked up at the clear blue sky. 'Doc, just now, that flash of light—'

'That was my handiwork, yes,' he admitted, leading them back down toward the tumbledown remains of the old mine head. 'I inserted a program meme into the Clade systems just before I disconnected myself from it to neutralise the memory transfer from—' The Doctor glanced at Nathan and saw that the boy hadn't understood a word he was saying. 'I made the bad dreams vanish,' he continued. 'If I did it right, the pulse will reach for miles in every direction, and hopefully touch everyone that Alvin Godlove healed. No more nightmares…' He blew out a breath. 'Well, at least no more *alien* ones. Can't really help you with the normal human kind.'

Nathan smiled. 'Oh, I reckon you have, Doc. I get the feelin' as long as you're around, nothing will ever seem scary again.'

As the evening drew in, they buried Walking Crow by the mine and Martha shed a few tears for him as the Doctor spoke in the Pawnee's tribal language, calling for the Great Spirit to watch over him and thank him for his sacrifice.

Then, with Nathan guiding them once more, they made their way back to Ironhill where a wary citizenry were waiting for them. The Doctor organised hotel rooms for the three of them and, more importantly, a bath. Nathan later remarked that he'd washed off enough mud to coat the roof of the schoolhouse, and Martha had to admit she hadn't been that grubby since Leo had pushed her in the river when they were kids.

The Doctor sat out on the balcony of the hotel where they stayed, watching the stars all night long. Martha and Nathan slept, and they did not dream at all.

TWENTY-ONE

Jenny Forrest and the recently appointed Sheriff Loomis Teague greeted them a day later, the three of them back in Redwater to a hero's welcome.

'I knew you were coming back,' Jenny explained, as they walked toward the alley where the TARDIS stood. 'There was this strange summer lightning in the sky, and after it passed...' She trailed off. 'I knew you had saved us.'

Teague nodded. 'Doc, I won't pretend to know what kinda mumbo-jumbo took place hereabouts, but I'd be a fool if I said we didn't all owe you our lives.'

The Doctor gave a wan smile. 'You know, Nathan's the real hero here.' He gestured to where the teenager was talking animatedly to Zachariah Hawkes and Joe Pitt. 'That young man faced a very difficult choice... and he made the right one.'

'I'll see to him,' promised Jenny. 'He has no blood

relatives still living, but the townsfolk will treat him like family.'

Martha nodded. 'That's good to know. And how about you?'

Jenny gave a sideways glance to Teague that was loaded with subtle signals, and Martha had to bite her lip.

'I have… friends,' said the schoolteacher. 'For all the horrors of the past days, the experience has brought us all closer together. Redwater is more a community now than it ever was.'

Teague nodded. 'You were right, Doc. We stood together.' He extended a hand and the Doctor shook it. 'You and Miss Jones, you're welcome in this town anytime the winds blow you back this way.' He tapped a finger to the brim of his hat and then walked away, his spurs clicking behind him.

The Doctor chuckled. 'Hard to believe he's the same guy who was cheating at cards and skimming off the ante a few days ago.'

'But you saw the potential in him,' said Jenny. 'I think you do that with everyone you meet, Doctor.' Martha saw the teacher watching her, and the other woman looked sad. 'And now you're both going to leave us,' she said.

Martha nodded, trying to keep a light tone to her voice. 'Places to go, people to see.'

'Best this way,' said the Doctor. 'I hate long goodbyes, don't you?'

'Hey, Doc!' As the three of them approached the police box, Nathan came bounding up to them. 'Hey, uh, listen. Mr Hawkes tells me my pa left the house to me and all…' He chewed his lip. 'I was thinkin', you and Miss Martha might want to stay a while?' He nodded at the TARDIS. 'A lot more room than in there, I'd reckon.'

'You'd be surprised,' Martha smiled.

'That's a kind offer, but we've got to move on.' The Doctor had the hat that Mr Vogel had given him in his hand, and he flipped it around his wrist and placed it on Nathan's head. 'Look after this for me, will you?'

'Sure,' said the youth, nodding reluctantly.

As Martha unlocked the TARDIS door, the Doctor gave Jenny a hopeful look. 'One last thing. Just for the sake of propriety, could you do me a favour and make sure Mr Hawkes back there keeps us out of his newspaper? I think history can roll on just fine without us cropping up where we shouldn't be.'

'I'll do that,' Jenny promised, 'but I'd beg to differ. History needs all the help it can get.'

The Doctor gave her a final nod and followed Martha into the TARDIS and shut the door behind him, closing off an all-too-brief glimpse of a strange, impossible room ranged inside.

For a long moment, Jenny and Nathan stood watching in silence; then the youth spoke. 'So, uh, what happens now? Is that shack there gonna sprout wheels and roll away?'

Jenny smiled ruefully. 'Given what I've seen of the Doctor, anything is possible.'

Abruptly the door opened a crack and the Doctor leaned out with a book in his hand. 'Jenny! Almost forgot, I have something for you. You liked Jules Verne, right? You're going to love this guy, then. Bit political at times, but some brilliant stories.'

He pressed the book into her hand and the teacher opened it at the first page. '*The Time Machine*,' she read aloud, '*An Invention*. By H.G. Wells.' Jenny saw something in the text and frowned. 'How odd. That must be a misprint. The publication date is ten years hence.'

'Yes, must be,' agreed the Doctor. 'I wouldn't go lending it to anyone else, though. Well, maybe Nathan... But when you've read it, things will make a bit more sense, I promise.' He smiled again. 'Bye!'

He left them there in silence; then the sound of mighty engines of infinity wheezed into action, and the TARDIS vanished into the fading light of the sunset.

Inside the time ship, the Doctor circled the central console and fiddled with the controls, patting and tapping the machine as one might stroke a cat, while the central column rose and fell, rose and fell.

Martha jerked her head in the direction of the doors. 'Was that a sensible thing to do, giving Jenny a copy of a book that hasn't even been written yet?'

'Ah, it's OK,' he said airily. 'I mean, what's she going

to do? It's not like she can post spoilers on the internet, is it?'

'Good point,' she agreed. Martha's fingers strayed to the hem of her leather jacket and she suddenly realised she was toying with the spot where Tangleleg's energy blast had hit her. She drew in a sharp breath, and from the corner of her eye she saw the Doctor pause.

'I'm glad you're all right,' he told her, the mirth fading for a moment. 'I'm only sorry it wasn't enough. There's always some who slip away… The Sheriff, Walking Crow, Alvin Godlove…'

'Him?' Martha blinked. 'But he was a scumbag!'

'Really?' The Doctor eyed her. 'Have you forgotten about all the people that man cured of smallpox, and who knows what other illnesses while he was carrying the Clade? I know he was motivated by greed, but a life saved is still a life saved.'

Martha paused, mulling it over. Perhaps the Doctor was right. Godlove had just been a quack con-artist with loose morals; she shuddered to think what could have happened if someone *really* dangerous, a true killer, had found the Clade in the woods that night.

'In his own warped sort of way, Alvin Godlove was trying to do the right thing. He was just… too weak to stand up to it.' She heard him sigh. 'The Clades have the power to heal or to kill.' He looked at the holster still belted around his waist and with a frown, he took it off and put it aside. 'Any kind of technology, it's always the same. It's not black or white, good or evil. It's how you use it, the intention behind it, that's the important thing.'

'Peacemakers,' said Martha, thinking.

'Yes,' replied the Doctor. After a moment, he crossed to where he'd dumped his brown coat in a heap on the chair and dipped into a pocket, his hand returning with her cell phone. His expression was troubled. 'I… I thought you might want this back.' He tossed it and Martha caught it out of the air. 'Just in case, y'know, if you wanted to call home.'

Martha opened the phone and her finger hovered over the keys. Whenever she had a bad experience in the past, it was Tish that she called, Tish who she moaned to, Tish that listened to her cry when she was dumped or just emotional over something. Martha thought about those moments after she had been injured, thinking of her family and wanting to see them again.

But what could she tell her sister if she called her? *I'm just phoning from the Wild West to tell you how I got zapped by a space alien super gun with a mind of its own.* She gave a slight shake of her head and snapped the phone shut again.

The Doctor was still watching her. 'After what happened, I wouldn't mind if you wanted to, you know… call it a day.'

'Call it a day?' Martha repeated. 'You mean, go home?' She nodded at the door again. 'Are you throwing me out?'

'What?' The Doctor was abashed. 'No, never. You're

a brilliant house guest. You do your share of the washing up and you don't leave dirty kilts everywhere, not like *some* people.' He paused, taking a breath. 'It's not that at all. I meant go home if *you* want to,' he said, without weight. 'It's not all fun and games, is it? It's risky, being a wanderer in the fourth dimension. I'd totally understand if you'd had enough, if all that was too much for you.' He sighed. 'It's not every day you stare death in the face. I'm sorry that had to happen to you, Martha, I really am.'

'It's not the first time I've been there recently. And if I stay, it could happen again, couldn't it?'

'Yes,' he admitted, careful and serious. 'It could. And the next time you might not be so lucky.'

A slow smile crossed her face, turning into a grin as the Doctor's expression became one of mild confusion. 'You know what? I lived through that. Me, Martha Jones, Medical Student. I lived through it and I was never afraid, not even for a second. Do you know why?'

He was starting to smile again. 'Tell me,' he said.

'Because I trust you. You're the Doctor.'

He shook his head and chuckled. 'And you're a rare one, Martha Jones.'

'I am,' she agreed, walking across to lean over his shoulder and study the monitor screen. 'So,' she asked, 'where next?'

The Doctor matched her grin. 'Let's follow the trails of time, and see where that takes us…'

* * *

ACKNOWLEDGEMENTS

My thanks to all these folks in the many domains of *Doctor Who* for their support and confidence:

Justin Richards and Russell T Davies for giving me the opportunity to tell a Tenth Doctor story.

John Ainsworth, Nick Briggs, Sharon Gosling, Simon Guerrier, Jason Haigh-Ellery, Alan Barnes and everyone else in the Big Finish crew.

Keith Topping, David McIntee, David Howe, Ben Aaronovitch, Marc Platt, Joe Lidster, Nick Wallace, Steven Savile, David Bishop, Andrew Cartmel, Paul Cornell, Caroline Symcox, Tony and Jane Kenealy, Shaun Lyon, Clay Eichelberger, Tara O'Shea, Jill Sherwin, Kathryn Sullivan, Stewart Vandal and David Gould for counsel and comradeship.

Sting of the Zygons

by *Stephen Cole*

ISBN 978 1 84607 225 3
UK £6.99 US $11.99/$14.99 CDN

The TARDIS lands the Doctor and Martha in the
Lake District in 1909, where a small village has been
terrorised by a giant, scaly monster. The search is on
for the elusive 'Beast of Westmorland', and explorers,
naturalists and hunters from across the country are
descending on the fells. King Edward VII himself is
on his way to join the search, with a knighthood for
whoever finds the Beast.

But there is a more sinister presence at work in the
Lakes than a mere monster on the rampage, and the
Doctor is soon embroiled in the plans of an old and
terrifying enemy. As the hunters become the hunted, a
desperate battle of wits begins – with the future of the
entire world at stake…

Also available from BBC Books
featuring the Doctor and Martha
as played by David Tennant and Freema Agyeman:

The Last Dodo

by Jacqueline Rayner
ISBN 978 1 84607 224 6
UK £6.99 US $11.99/$14.99 CDN

The Doctor and Martha go in search of a real live dodo,
and are transported by the TARDIS to the mysterious
Museum of the Last Ones. There, in the Earth section,
they discover every extinct creature up to the present
day, all still alive and in suspended animation.

Preservation is the museum's only job – collecting
the last of every endangered species from all over the
universe. But exhibits are going missing…

Can the Doctor solve the mystery before the museum's
curator adds the last of the Time Lords to her
collection?

Wooden Heart

by Martin Day

ISBN 978 1 84607 226 0

UK £6.99 US $11.99/$14.99 CDN

A vast starship, seemingly deserted and spinning slowly in the void of deep space. Martha and the Doctor explore this drifting tomb, and discover that they may not be alone after all…

Who survived the disaster that overcame the rest of the crew? What continues to power the vessel? And why has a stretch of wooded countryside suddenly appeared in the middle of the craft?

As the Doctor and Martha journey through the forest, they find a mysterious, fogbound village – a village traumatised by missing children and prophecies of its own destruction.

DOCTOR·WHO

Forever Autumn
by Mark Morris
ISBN 978 1 84607 270 3
UK £6.99 US $11.99/$14.99 CDN

It is almost Halloween in the sleepy New England town of Blackwood Falls. Autumn leaves litter lawns and sidewalks, paper skeletons hang in windows, and carved pumpkins leer from stoops and front porches.

The Doctor and Martha soon discover that something long dormant has awoken in the town, and this will be no ordinary Halloween. What is the secret of the ancient tree and the mysterious book discovered tangled in its roots? What rises from the local churchyard in the dead of night, sealing up the lips of the only witness? And why are the harmless trappings of Halloween suddenly taking on a creepy new life of their own?

As nightmarish creatures prowl the streets, the Doctor and Martha must battle to prevent both the townspeople and themselves from suffering a grisly fate…

DOCTOR·WHO

Sick Building

by Paul Magrs

ISBN 978 1 84607 269 7

UK £6.99 US $11.99/$14.99 CDN

Tiermann's World: a planet covered in wintry woods
and roamed by sabre-toothed tigers and other
savage beasts. The Doctor is here to warn Professor
Tiermann, his wife and their son that a terrible danger
is on its way.

The Tiermanns live in luxury, in a fantastic, futuristic,
fully automated Dreamhome, under an impenetrable
force shield. But that won't protect them from the
Voracious Craw. A gigantic and extremely hungry alien
creature is heading remorselessly towards their home.
When it gets there everything will be devoured.

Can they get away in time? With the force shield
cracking up, and the Dreamhome itself deciding who
should or should not leave, things are
looking desperate…

Wetworld

by Mark Michalowski

ISBN 978 1 84607 271 0

UK £6.99 US $11.99/$14.99 CDN

When the TARDIS makes a disastrous landing in the
swamps of the planet Sunday, the Doctor has no choice
but to abandon Martha and try to find help. But the
tranquillity of Sunday's swamps is deceptive, and even
the TARDIS can't protect Martha forever.

The human pioneers of Sunday have their own dangers
to face: homeless and alone, they're only just starting to
realise that Sunday's wildlife isn't as harmless as it first
seems. Why are the native otters behaving so strangely,
and what is the creature in the swamps that is so
interested in the humans, and the new arrivals?

The Doctor and Martha must fight to ensure that
human intelligence doesn't become the greatest danger
of all.

Wishing Well

by Trevor Baxendale

ISBN 978 1 84607 348 9

UK £6.99 US $11.99/$14.99 CDN

The old village well is just a curiosity – something to attract tourists intrigued by stories of lost treasure, or visitors just making a wish. Unless something alien and terrifying could be lurking inside the well? Something utterly monstrous that causes nothing but death and destruction?

But who knows the real truth about the well? Who wishes to unleash the hideous force it contains? What terrible consequences will follow the search for a legendary treasure hidden at the bottom?

No one wants to believe the Doctor's warnings about the deadly horror lying in wait – but soon they'll wish they had…

The Pirate Loop

by Simon Guerrier

ISBN 978 1 84607 347 2
UK £6.99 US $11.99/$14.99 CDN

The Doctor's been everywhere and everywhen in
the whole of the universe and seems to know all the
answers. But ask him what happened to the Starship
Brilliant and he hasn't the first idea. Did it fall into
a sun or black hole? Was it shot down in the first
moments of the galactic war? And what's this about a
secret experimental drive?

The Doctor is skittish. But if Martha is so keen to find
out he'll land the TARDIS on the *Brilliant*, a few days
before it vanishes. Then they can see for themselves…

Soon the Doctor learns the awful truth. And Martha
learns that you need to be careful what you wish for.
She certainly wasn't hoping for mayhem, death, and
badger-faced space pirates.

DOCTOR · WHO

The Inside Story

by Gary Russell

ISBN 978 0 56348 649 7

£14.99

In March 2005, a 900-year-old alien in a police public call box made a triumphant return to our television screens. *The Inside Story* takes us behind the scenes to find out how the series was commissioned, made and brought into the twenty-first century. Gary Russell has talked extensively to everyone involved in the show, from the Tenth Doctor himself, David Tennant, and executive producer Russell T Davies, to the people normally hidden inside monster suits or behind cameras. Everyone has an interesting story to tell.

The result is the definitive account of how the new *Doctor Who* was created. With exclusive access to design drawings, backstage photographs, costume designs and other previously unpublished pictures, *The Inside Story* covers the making of all twenty-six episodes of Series One and Two, plus the Christmas specials, as well as an exclusive look ahead to the third series.

DOCTOR·WHO

Creatures and Demons
by Justin Richards
ISBN 978 1 84607 229 1
UK £7.99 US $12.99/$15.99 CDN

Throughout his many adventures in time and space, the Doctor has encountered aliens, monsters, creatures and demons from right across the universe. In this third volume of alien monstrosities and dastardly villains, *Doctor Who* expert and acclaimed author Justin Richards describes some of the evils the Doctor has fought in over forty years of time travel.

From the grotesque Abzorbaloff to the monstrous Empress of the Racnoss, from giant maggots to the Daleks of the secret Cult of Skaro, from the Destroyer of Worlds to the ancient Beast itself… This book brings together more of the terrifying enemies the Doctor has battled against.

Illustrated throughout with stunning photographs and design drawings from the current series of *Doctor Who* and his previous 'classic' incarnations, this book is a treat for friends of the Doctor whatever their age, and whatever planet they come from…

DOCTOR·WHO

Starships and Spacestations

by Justin Richards
ISBN 978 1 84607 423 3
£7.99 US $12.99/$15.99 CDN

The Doctor has his TARDIS to get him from place to
place and time to time, but the rest of the Universe
relies on more conventional transport… From the
British Space Programme of the late twentieth century
to Earth's Empire in the far future, from the terrifying
Dalek Fleet to deadly Cyber Ships, this book documents
the many starships and spacestations that the Doctor
and his companions have encountered on their travels.

He has been held prisoner in space, escaped from the
moon, witnessed the arrival of the Sycorax and the
crash landing of a space pig… More than anyone else,
the Doctor has seen the development of space travel
between countless worlds.

This stunningly illustrated book tells the amazing story
of Earth's ventures into space, examines the many alien
fleets who have paid Earth a visit, and explores the
other starships and spacestations that the Doctor has
encountered on his many travels…